MILES LEDOUX

MEMORY LANE

Winter in Veil, Book 10

Prologue

Violet could feel the man's thick, strong hands crushing her windpipe. She clawed at his arm, kicked at his midsection, but he was twice her size and he shook her like a rag doll. There was no way she could escape. His hands would stay fastened around her throat for the rest of her life—which probably wouldn't be more than another few seconds. This was to be her end, death by strangulation. That or blunt-force trauma, as he began to crack the back of her head against a wooden pillar over and over.

The pain was excruciating. She tried to replace the awful sensations dominating her last moments with thoughts of those she loved: Cyanne, Jen, Candy—

Violet's mind reeled. She and Candy would never have the chance to reconcile! She couldn't die like this, with things so unresolved, her business unfinished...

Am I going to come back as a ghost?

No! Violet tried to will her limbs into action. There must be a way to fight back, there must be...! But her body was beginning to lose feeling. Her vision, too, was dimming. The last thing she saw was the shiny badge worn by her murderer...

There was a thunderous noise, like an explosion, and suddenly Violet was free. She dropped to the floor unceremoniously. Coughing, she scrambled away from her attacker, knowing she was cutting her palms on the shattered glass spread across the floor—except she felt nothing slicing into her skin, only the floor's smooth wood paneling. She flipped onto her back, ready to fend off her attacker as he came after her—

He wasn't there. She twisted her head one way, then the other. She knew he was about to spring out of nowhere and finish what he'd started. Wobbily she got to her feet and tried to spot him…but he didn't appear to be in the store. Had he run off? Had he given up waiting for Violet to asphyxiate, and fled?

Violet's chest heaved as she caught her breath, and she realized with a start that rather than aching, as it had a moment ago, her throat felt fine. Her head, likewise, felt undamaged. *Must be adrenaline,* she thought.

What had caused that loud noise? Was it a gunshot? Why hadn't it brought anyone running? For that matter, why hadn't the *first* gunshot—

Violet gasped. *"Joy!!"* She ran out from the aisle to where her friend and employer had fallen behind the cash register after taking a bullet.

But she wasn't there. No blood, no body.

As Violet stood there in shock, other curious details began to register. The glass on the floor had not cut her because the floor was clean. The mess caused by the fight had completely disappeared. Not only that, when the fight had happened, it was late afternoon. The light pouring through the store windows was that of was mid-morning.

"What…the hell?" Violet stood there, perplexed, and then jumped as the door opened and a customer entered.

She jumped again at yet another shock: Joy Dosley, smiling and perfectly healthy, emerged from the back room.

"Joy! Oh my god!" Joy was one of the only adults in Veil who was shorter than Violet; to give her a bear hug risked smothering her, but Violet was so happy to see her she decided it was worth it, and threw open her arms—

"Hello, sir, can I help you?"

If Violet was stunned that Joy completely ignored her presence, she was even more stunned when she saw who the customer was. "Well, that depends," said the oily voice of Henry Glass as he approached the register. He was even wearing the same suit as the day Violet first met him. "I'm new in town," he said, "and I'm not entirely sure I'm in the right place."

"What do you mean, new in town?!" snapped Violet, though he, too, ignored her.

Joy said, "Well, I'm happy to—oh, damn, the delivery's here. Violet?"

"Wha…?" Violet was so confused.

"Would you help this gentleman while I take a delivery?"

A voice called, "Yeah, sure!"

Violet felt a shiver creep all the way up her back…

As another Violet emerged from among the shelves and took Joy's place at the register. "How can I help you?"

Violet felt dizzy. She put a hand to her head. "Oh no," she moaned. "No, not again…"

* * *

"She's got a pulse!"

Bruises covered Violet's throat. Blood matted her hair. Paramedics swarmed about her unconscious body until they loaded her into an ambulance alongside Joy, and took them away.

The man who had tried to kill them was taken away later, inside a black bag.

I

It occurred to Cyanne Grogan, as she bit into the fish sandwich, that she hadn't eaten since early this morning. Only now did she discover just how hungry she was. As the hunger dissipated, the day's events began to fall into better perspective.

To start with, there had been the heart-stopping moment when her boyfriend, Luther, had appeared to be guilty of abduction and attempted rape, but of course that had proven to be a misunderstanding. Cy's relief had been immense—and she realized, looking back, that she'd been holding her breath, in a sense, for over two months. Ever since the bombshell discovery that her father had disowned and abandoned her on the pretext that she was a danger to him, Cy's ability to trust people had suffered. She hadn't seen his betrayal coming at all...so what was coming next? Or rather, *who*—who would be the next to betray and hurt her?

It had seemed the answer would be Luther...and then that awful moment was over. All was well. She was safe. Her fear was proven unjustified. She could relax.

Then, all of a sudden, Luther had broken up with her.

And right after that had come the email.

Several weeks ago, Cy had had a falling out with two school

friends, Em and Neesha, and she wanted to reconnect with them. Last night she'd sent them an invitation.

Neesha's response was a harsh message with an extraordinary claim—and an attached document to prove it.

To some, Cy reflected, it might seem as if she'd overreacted by deciding to run away. But they couldn't understand. They just *couldn't understand.* She *had* to run away. Because not running away meant staying there. With *her.*

Yes, running away was hell.

The alternative was something worse.

She'd packed up some essentials, gotten cash from where her mother kept an emergency stash, bought a bus ticket online, and set out on foot for the bus station. She'd work out a final destination later. For now, her only goal was escape. Escape before another betrayal came and finished her off.

Cy felt no emotion as the bus drove out of Veil, no sentimental urge to take one last look at the town that was her home. Feelings were dangerous, and she was done with them. She didn't care if she never felt anything again. Hell, if she never cared, period, then she'd never have to worry about being hurt.

Right about then came the radio report, in the deep voice of anchor Rod Piper, of the shooting that had just occurred in the Dosleys' store.

Joy Dosley and her family lived next door to Cy and her mother (and Violet, since she'd come to stay with them). Recently, Cy had become friends with Joy's teenage daughter, Kristy. Joy ran a small store on Main Street called 'Tis the Seasoning. After coming to live with the Grogans, Violet had taken a job in the store.

The *basso profundo* voice blaring across the bus's interior reported that while details were unclear, it was confirmed that a shooting had occurred less than an hour ago, and that Joy and Violet had been injured...and Sheriff Dubowski was dead.

The bus's first stop was in Platte, the tiny hamlet just outside Veil. Cy all but leaped off the bus, but then she faltered. Violet was a dear friend—perhaps her best friend—and Cy very much wanted to go to the hospital and be there for her.

But she could *not stay.*

She hadn't even said *goodbye* to Violet. She'd left a short note for her mother, but—

No, she couldn't stay! She *couldn't!*

Somewhere amidst the inner turmoil, Cy registered that she was freezing. Late January and early February were the coldest weeks in Vermont. She stepped into the Platte café and ordered a sandwich.

Her belly full, Cy was able to think a little more clearly. Able to see how much she'd been pretending the last two months, how much she'd wanted to believe things were okay between her mother and her, when all the time she'd been waiting for the other shoe to drop, preparing for the worst. The tension was exhausting, eating away at her sanity.

Perhaps she *was* acting too hastily.

The anxious thoughts shouted again, only they seemed to shout from farther away. There would be another bus leaving Veil later, but Cy was undecided on whether to take it. Perhaps she didn't need to run after all. Truth be told, she didn't want to. What if Violet needed her? At the very least, Cy needed to know if she'd be okay.

Cy folded her arms on the table and laid down her head. She had to make a decision. What was holding her back?

The image of the document on her phone screen reared its ugly head.

Was it possible Neesha was lying? Would she go to the trouble of faking a document like that? Cy had a strong feeling it was real...

Was there any way to be sure?

Cy lifted her head. *There might be.*

She left the café, regretted not having her bicycle with her, and headed for a certain house on the outskirts of Veil.

* * *

"It all came out of nowhere," said Joy. The painkillers made her sound dazed. She lay in a hospital bed with her arm in a sling. Fran Dosley sat next to her, holding her hand. Their daughter Kristy had been sent home with the baby.

"Who entered the store first?" asked Jen, giving Joy a place to start. She'd already heard Joy's story back at the crime scene, but she'd asked her to tell it again, now that things had calmed down. Deputies Derrick and Hayden stood by the door, listening. To Jen they weren't fellow deputies anymore. They were *her* deputies. Sheriff Grogan. Sheriff...

She'd deal with all of that later.

"I didn't see Violet come in," Joy said in her monotone, "but I think she must've come in after the sheriff."

"What did Dubowski do?"

"He brought some things to the register and paid for them."

"Did he say anything?"

"We talked about the two young men who are suspected of abducting Bethany Williams. Well, I guess *I* was doing most of the talking."

"Did Sheriff Dubowski seem distracted? Worried?"

"I guess he might not have been too interested in what I was babbling about, but I don't think he had anything on his mind."

"What happened after he paid?"

"He left."

Sheriff Grogan narrowed her eyes. "He left the store? Do you mean he left and then came back?"

For a moment Joy seemed to have drifted off. She was staring off into space. "No…he didn't leave. But I thought he was going to. I put his receipt with the others, and when I looked up, he was still standing there, with his back to me. He and Violet were staring at each other."

"Were they talking?"

"No. Just staring. Violet had this…this look on her face. Like she'd seen a ghost. Or something worse."

"All right. What happened next?"

"Well, that's when he shot me." Joy let go of Fran and touched her injured arm.

Grogan blinked. "He and Violet were staring at each other… and he just—shot you?"

Joy nodded.

"He didn't say or do anything just before that?"

"That's what she just told you," said Fran, her voice mild but her eyes flashing dangerously.

"Now, wait," said Derrick, stepping forward. "A shooting incident can be very upsetting. Maybe your memory is a little fuzzy."

"Deputy," said Grogan warningly.

"Are you sure the sheriff didn't start arguing with Violet, and then—"

"No," Joy said mildly, shaking her head. "He just pulled out his gun and—oh, wait, there was something just before that."

"What?" demanded Grogan.

"I asked Violet what was wrong. Because of how scared she looked."

Jen frowned to herself.

"And that's when he pulled out his gun. He tried to shoot me in the chest, but Violet shoved him, so he hit me in the arm instead."

Derrick scoffed, "Oh, give me a break."

"Deputy, you can wait outside," Grogan ordered.

Joy blithely continued, "And then Violet tried to get away, but he grabbed her, so she knocked the gun out of his hand."

"That's not possible," Hayden said firmly.

Grogan shouted, "Both of you—out!"

"And then he…he strangled…" Joy's lip trembled. Fran held her as she broke down in sobs. "He killed her. He killed her right in front of me. My arm was hurting—I couldn't get to the gun in time." She let out a mournful wail.

Grogan stepped forward and took Joy's hand. "Joy, listen. Listen to me. Violet is alive."

Joy gasped. "She is?!"

"Yes, she's alive. Dubowski didn't kill her."

"You *saved* her," Fran added, shooting a momentary glance of reproach at Grogan, as if to say, *You should have told her that.*

* * *

Out in the hall, Grogan took the deputies down three doors before she snapped, "Decide right now—are you going to act like deputies, or do I have to send you home?"

"You can't believe all that garbage!" hissed Deputy Derrick. "The sheriff would never draw his weapon without cause, let alone—"

"The sheriff trained us to follow the evidence in an investigation. That's our job. And so far all the evidence bears out Joy's story. We know Dubowski fired that first shot into her arm. If Violet were awake, we could ask her—"

"Well, she's not. So what do we tell the public?"

"We can't let that woman paint the sheriff as an attempted rapist and murderer," Hayden said darkly.

Grogan drew a breath and said quietly, "Hayden, go home."

Both Derrick and Hayden blinked. "What?"

"Go home. Right now. Without saying anything. Or I'm suspending you."

Hayden set off down the hall with a stunned look on her face.

Grogan turned to Derrick. "Anything to add, Deputy?"

"No...no, ma'am."

"Good. If anyone asks, our investigation is ongoing. We do not yet have an official statement as to what's happened. When we *have* an official statement, they'll know." She pointed back toward Joy's recovery room. "I want a deputy outside her door at all times. She doesn't move from that room without my knowing. No one speaks to her apart from family and hospital staff. Got it?"

Derrick barely managed a "Yes, ma'am" before she strode toward the exit. "Where are you going?" he called after her.

She paused and turned back. "It might help to know what exactly Violet was doing at that store. There's one person who I bet could tell us that."

"Who?"

"The last person she spoke to before she went there."

* * *

"Candy, I am so sorry."

When Violet opened her eyes and found herself no longer in Joy's store, for a moment she thought she'd woken up. But she soon recognized this was not the real world. This was another memory.

"I made a terrible mistake... I'm hoping you can forgive me."

10

There had been a previous occasion when Violet had, while unconscious, found herself in a hauntingly convincing dreamscape, which she'd promptly forgotten about once she'd woken up, just like any other dream. Now it came back to her clearly, as if she'd remembered it all along, and she wondered if perhaps it was more than a dream. That last time, the location hadn't been a memory but an illusion, a place she'd never been before, with a person who, as far as she knew, she'd never met...

April.

As unpleasant as that experience had been, she'd choose it in a heartbeat over reliving this argument. Even watching from the sidelines, it killed her to see Candy looking at her that way. It made her feel like the worst person in the world all over again.

"Candy," said the other Violet, the past Violet, *"I* want to be there for *you.* I know I let you down today, but—"

"Then why did you do it?!" Candy flung away the wet cloth she was holding. It flew straight into Violet's leg—the real Violet—but she was too upset to notice. "If you knew it would let me down, why did you leave? Why does everyone I love and trust turn out to be—"

Violet turned around and covered her ears. "This is why I have to wake up!" she told herself. "I have to make things right with her! I hurt her and it was my fault, but I'm going to make it better! Oh God, I wish I hadn't left her..." She shut her eyes tightly in remorse.

When she opened them, she found herself once more transported. Again, there was a double of herself, leaning against the wall by a window. The double was staring at something outside, her eyes widening in alarm.

This memory was from this morning, on the second story of the ice cream shop. Violet knew what was about to happen.

She whispered, "No…"

It was the moment before past-Violet made the decision she regretted, that would betray someone she loved.

Violet looked from herself to Candy in growing anguish, part of her sorely lamenting the fact that she could remember things in such acute detail.

"Violet," said Candy, "what's the matter?"

Past-Violet opened her mouth to respond.

"No, don't!" Violet shouted. "Don't do it! Just stay! The sheriff's fine—I mean, for now—but anyway he's not worth it! It's a waste! Please—don't go…"

"I—I have to go check something," said past-Violet.

And Violet watched, helpless, as her past self ran down the stairs, leaving Candy with an expression of hurt bewilderment. Violet moved toward her, knowing Candy couldn't see or hear her, that none of this was real. "I'm sorry," she sobbed. "I'm so sorry. If I could just undo it…" She wiped her eyes.

All at once, she was outside. Stumbling, she tried to get her bearings. She recognized Platte's main intersection. The last time she'd been here was when—

Violet spotted herself as she trod, as if hypnotized, toward the woods at the end of a certain dead-end road.

"No!" Violet shouted, darting forward.

It's not real, said a voice within her.

But Violet couldn't help herself. "Don't go in!! Don't do it!! Stop!! You don't know what's in there!!"

You can't change what happened.

"Please!" Violet begged. "You're gonna get kidnapped! And because of that, Cy's gonna get kidnapped, too!"

She looked on helplessly as past-Violet vanished into the trees.

Violet sank to her knees, tilted her head back and appealed to the nonexistent sky. "Please stop this. Please let me out. Don't make me relive the choices I can't undo. If I can't change what I did, then at least don't make me watch. Please…"

Taking a deep breath, she shut her eyes.

II

"Who is it?" called Candy in response to the knock. The door must have garbled the reply, for it sounded like, "It's Dep—it's Sher—it's Jen Grogan." Candy was staying in a room at the bed and breakfast. She opened the door and regarded Jen blearily.

"Well, you're looking better," Jen remarked. The last time she'd seen her, Candy's eyes had been bloodshot from having been hit in the face with pepper spray. The redness and swelling had almost gone away.

"I took an acetaminophen and slept," said Candy.

Jen nodded, then said, "Candy, I need to talk to you."

Even in this state, Candy was perceptive. "What's wrong?"

Jen took her inside and they both sat down. "Violet was attacked," she said. "She's in the hospital."

"W-what?"

"She was concussed pretty badly. For a while she was in a coma, but now she's just sleeping."

Candy was clearly spinning into a panic. "Is she gonna be all right? She's not—"

"The doctors think she'll be okay. They're not sure when she's going to wake up, but they insisted she be allowed to do it on her own. That's why I can't question her."

14

Candy needed a minute to regain her self-control, and Jen gave her that minute in silence. Wiping away a tear, Candy asked quietly, "Who did it?"

"That's what I need your help to verify. Candy, what did you and Violet talk about when you last saw her?"

A pained expression came over Candy. "I—shouted at her. I was... My eyes were hurting so badly and I was just so angry, I didn't—I didn't mean to..."

Jen patted her hand. "What were you angry about?"

Candy swallowed. "We were in the ice cream shop, waiting to trap the man who'd assaulted Bethany, just like we'd planned. All of a sudden, Violet said she had to go do something—and she left. Even though it risked ruining the plan, she ran outside."

Jen frowned. "What did she have to do?"

"She wouldn't tell me. At least, not at first. Later she said she'd thought someone's life was in danger, but she was wrong."

"Where did she run to?"

"I'm not sure. Out in back of the building, I think. Toward Dime Road." She looked up at Jen appealingly. "She's—really going to be okay, right? I shouldn't have... The last thing I said to her was..."

"Take a deep breath." Once Candy had complied, Jen said, "Now, I want you to think carefully. Did Violet see something that made her run outside?"

"Maybe... Wait, yes, she did. Out the window."

"Which window?"

"The side window. Wait, no. She was at the side window, but she was looking at me. I was at the back window." Candy's eyes widened. "That's it. She looked past me, out the back window, and she looked...startled. When I looked out, I didn't see anything."

"And she said she thought someone's life was in danger?"

Candy nodded. "She didn't say whose."

Jen stood up. "Thank you, Candy." Before leaving, she added, "If you want to sit with Violet in the hospital, I'll make sure you're allowed." Halfway out the door, she doubled back. "And if you find Cy there, tell her to call me back. I need to know where she is."

* * *

Cy was, at that moment, ringing the doorbell of a small house on the edge of town. Footsore, she shifted her weight from side to side, sucking in air through her teeth. She reflected that Myrna Redpath, her mother's old friend and schoolmate, so seldom received any visitors that there was a slight chance she'd forgotten what the ringing noise signified. Nevertheless, the door opened and Myrna stood before her, clad in a holey sweatshirt and smelling of…something that Cy felt she'd be best not knowing what. "Hi," she said as a preamble.

Myrna surveyed Cy's luggage and, without waiting for Cy to go on, said, "You can sleep on the couch. Blankets in the back."

"What? Oh—no, I didn't come to stay here."

Myrna raised an eyebrow and jerked her head at the luggage. "You running away from home?"

Cy remembered that, while eccentric, Myrna could some-times be very sharp. "I want to talk to you about my mom."

Myrna grunted and shuffled away. Cy took that as an invitation to come in.

Knives and other sharp instruments covered most every surface in the house. Strangely, the only place that seemed to be devoid of pointy objects was the kitchen counter. Cy set down her belongings and followed Myrna toward the refrigerator.

"You want something to drink?" asked Myrna.

"No, thank you."

Myrna opened the fridge. "I have orange juice, cranberry juice, and some stuff Hal Clayton gave me. I haven't tried it yet; maybe you could tell me if it's good."

"No, no, I'm okay, thank you." Cy drew a quick breath. "When I was born, my family was still living here in Veil. Were you and Mom talking back then?

Myrna shrugged, taking out the thermos given to her by Hal Clayton. "I guess."

"What I mean is…did she tell you things?"

"What things?" Myrna sniffed at the thermos's contents.

"Like, personal things. Really personal."

"Is this about your dad?" Myrna still seemed focused on the thermos. "Are you wondering if your mom cheated on your dad? You think maybe he's not your real dad?"

Cy did a double take. "Is—he not?"

"No, he is. I just wondered if that's what you were wondering."

Cy put a hand over her eyes. "Myrna…"

Ughh! Myrna had tried Hal's concoction. She spat the contents into the sink. "What the balls?!"

"Myrna!" Cy stepped forward. "I need to ask you… Did my mom—want me?"

Myrna was still spitting. "Did she want you to what?"

"Did she want—to have me?"

"Of course she wanted to have you."

"She never—changed her mind about having me?"

"Well, obviously. You're here, aren't you?"

Cy turned a sickly color. "What if that's only because she had to?"

Wiping her mouth, Myrna paused. Finally her attention seemed to narrow on Cy. "What do you mean?"

"What if she didn't want to have me...but was forced to?"

"Who told you that?"

"I saw a document. The year I was born, my mom wanted to have an abortion."

"You—*saw* a document?"

Cy sighed. "My classmate showed it to me."

"And you believe this 'classmate?' They're a friend? Someone you trust?"

"I wouldn't exactly say we're friends, but—"

"So they showed you this document to try to hurt you. You're believing this person who's trying to hurt you—instead of trusting your mother?"

Cy looked up angrily. "That's not—I—you don't—"

Myrna picked at her teeth with a fingernail.

Cy reined herself in and said tightly, "I just wanted to know if you knew whether my mother tried to have an abortion."

"Of course I did."

Cy paled. "Then—it's true! She—didn't want me."

Myrna shook her head. "Nah, of course she wanted you."

Cy barely kept her temper. "Look, I'm trying to make up my mind about a big decision here. So could you please not mess with me?"

Myrna looked her in the eye. "If you're gonna run away, then run away. Just know that once you do, it's not saying something about your ma. It's saying something about *you*." She grabbed up the thermos and held it out to Cy. "Now take this and go talk to your ma."

Cy deflated and shook her head. Coming here had been a mistake. She started gathering up her belongings.

"No, no, no." Myrna waved her down. "You can leave your stuff here. Pick it up later."

18

"What?"

"Pick it up later, after you and your ma have worked things out."

Cy stared at her. Taking Myrna seriously was no easy feat—probably because Myrna went out of her way to let everyone know she didn't *care* whether they took her seriously or not. But, looking past her quirks, Myrna genuinely seemed to want to help Cy make peace with her mother.

More importantly, she seemed to think doing so was not only possible, but likely.

Slowly, Cy set her things down. "Okay. I'll try," she said. She headed for the door.

"Hey, don't forget this." Again, Myrna pushed the thermos toward her.

"Wait, why am I taking this?"

"Because I don't want it. You can give it to that 'classmate' of yours. What was their name?"

"Neesha, but—oh, fine." Cy took the thermos, making a mental note to drop it in the first waste bin she came across.

After Cy had left, Myrna murmured to herself, "Neesha..."

* * *

Jen couldn't help a twinge of emotion as she ascended the stairs to the second floor of the ice cream shop. Only a few hours ago, Sheriff Dubowski had climbed these same steps, doing his duty as sheriff and protector of Veil. He'd been Jen's hero and mentor for a long time. Now he was gone. And the person who'd taken his life claimed he died trying to commit a double murder—let alone the murder of someone she cared about a great deal.

Jen admitted to herself that if she hadn't heard Joy's story for herself, she'd likely have acted the same way that Deputy

Hayden had. Had benching her been the right call? With fewer deputies, her duties to the town were that much harder to fulfill. *Sheriff Jen Grogan.* The title made her feel bewildered. And proud. And a little bit sick. And, for now, very sad.

Jen leaned over and peered out the window Candy had described. It was dark now, but the streetlights had come on. Hopefully whatever Violet had seen could still be visible by—

A vehicle parked on Dime Road caught Jen's attention. A particular conversation flashed into her head, the last conversation she'd ever had with the man she most respected in Veil, perhaps in the world: *"Last night, I had a flat tire. I didn't have a spare, so I walked home and planned to get it fixed the next day."* Apparently the flat tire had happened there on Dime Road, and evidently Sheriff Dubowski had not had a chance to fix it.

Jen pulled out her radio. "Deputy Benno, come in."

"Go ahead."

Ten minutes later, Deputy Benno met the new sheriff on Dime Road. Benno handed Grogan the keys he'd taken from the old sheriff's desk. "Is that Dubowski's?" He pointed to the SUV with the flat tire.

Grogan unlocked the door and said, "I need you to stay while I search it."

"Search it for what?"

Jen didn't reply, though in just a couple of minutes, they had their answer. Having gone through the glove compartment, Jen opened the central armrest.

She froze and said, "Benno. Come here."

Somewhat reluctantly, Benno got in on the passenger side.

Both of them stared down at a cellular phone inside a case depicting the serene, haloed figure of Jesus Christ.

Benno looked up in shock and anguish.

It took every effort for Jen to remain stony-faced. She didn't speak a word as she bagged the phone as evidence.

* * *

She has to die.

She has. To. Die.

We've left her alone for far too long, and look what she's done!

I'll have to kill her, myself. No one else will.

They still have her in the hospital. Once they release her, it'll be so much harder to get to her.

I'll have to do it tonight. I WILL do it tonight.

She's not leaving that hospital alive.

III

Since waking up in Veil, Violet had discovered not only her ability to remember events perfectly, but also a keen perception of the passage of time. Whether or not she was paying attention to it, as long as she was awake, she could accurately determine the length of time between two events. Some days, she found this aspect rather vexing, like when she was in pain or waiting until a boring occasion had passed. Or when she was with Candy, and she wanted to make the seconds feel like hours, to make time stand still...

Here in this purgatory, however, she had absolutely no impression of passing time. She might have been traversing her memories for hours, or even days, she couldn't tell.

It was driving her insane.

"Help me!!" she hollered at the back of herself in her bedroom. The cat, Roswell, looking over past-Violet's shoulder, was the only one who seemed aware of her presence.

Moments later—or perhaps months—she was with another past Violet who was waiting for Cy outside a house in the country. "Help me," Violet begged. "Just look at me...please..."

Inside the house, Hal Clayton showed past-Violet an old photograph of Roberta Lammwych. Violet gazed at herself in desperation. She could try to touch her doppelgänger to

22

get her attention, but if these memories weren't real—or, in another sense, if *Violet* wasn't real—then her hand could pass right through herself. The idea made her skin crawl.

"Please!" Violet begged. "I'm trapped! Help me!" She put her mouth next to her twin's ear. "WHY CAN'T YOU HEAR ME?!"

Past-Violet squinted at the photograph.

It was hopeless. Why was she trying to reach her past self, anyway? What could she do? If Violet wasn't really here...or if *here* wasn't really *here,* then...

Violet sank to the floor. All that she'd truly wanted, she admitted to herself, was not to feel alone. If her life was ending, then she'd take that illusion over reminders of her failures. If only she could relive memories of closeness with people she loved and cared for: Cy, Jen, Benno, Candy...Trisha...

But she had no control. Her mind was a leaf in a whirlwind. Even if she found herself watching a happy event from her life, she might blink and it would be gone, never to be seen again.

"I'm going to die alone and lost," she said, hating how maudlin she sounded. "I'm not even going to find out who I really am." She hugged her legs and buried her face between her knees.

A soft breeze washed over her. Something tickled her hands. Slowly she looked up. She was sitting in the middle of a grassy field, not far from a dusty road. Everywhere was foliage the colors of fire: red, orange, gold.

For a moment Violet wasn't sure where she was, let alone when. Then she recognized the mountains on the edge of Veil. She was just outside the town.

"Wait a minute..." Was this the spot where—

Violet heard a strange sound and looked down. *A bloody hand reached toward her—*

With a yelp, she scrambled away and made it to her feet.

Shakily she turned and regarded the woman lying face down in the grass, a trail of blood running from her head to the large rock beside her.

It was Violet, of course. This was where she'd first woken up, the earliest memory she could access. Something catastrophic had happened to her here, had robbed her of her past and her identity. She hadn't visited this spot in months. It scared her too much.

Violet knelt beside the gasping creature, who made feeble attempts to push herself up from the ground. "What happened to you?" she asked her. "How did you get here? Where did you come from?"

And suddenly it hit her: could she find out, at last? Out in the real world she knew it wasn't possible, but in this dream-world the rules weren't so clearly defined. Wanting to know her identity had apparently brought her here. Was there a way she could go back farther, to her memories beyond this moment? So far her journey had been random, haphazard, but if she focused, concentrated hard enough...

It was worth a try.

She was momentarily glad she was all alone; given what she was about to do, any observer would question her sanity. She lay down on her stomach, copying her double's position. She tried to recall the searing pain, the wetness of the blood, the chill of the air.

"Who was I before this?" she whispered. "What brought me here?" She pressed her face into the grass till her eyes were forced to shut.

Something changed. She knew it instantly. The breeze was gone. The ground beneath her was flat and hard. She lifted her face. It was pavement. Night had fallen.

Violet got to her feet and looked around. She was in the middle of a parking lot. Her heart sank: she recognized it. Her attempt hadn't worked. She was still in Veil. The last time she'd been here was Halloween night. Any moment, she and Deputy Benno would arrive. He'd brought her here to help investigate the disappearance of—

"Seriously? You walked here?"

Violet spun around. *What the—?!?*

Rob Mulroy was giving her a quizzical look.

But it couldn't be Rob Mulroy, Cy's ex-boyfriend. He was dead. Violet had only ever met him twice, and neither of those occasions had taken place here. In fact, the only time she knew of Rob coming to this empty lot was when he—

"I've lived in Veil all my life."

Violet spun again. She beheld a much older man whom she'd never met in person but could recognize from photographs: Tuck Fleagle. "I know all the backyard alleys and shortcuts," he said. "Useful to a man who doesn't want to be followed."

Violet had heard this conversation before. She knew what was about to happen. *But I wasn't here!! I wasn't around when this happened! How can I be seeing it???*

"You think people are following you?" Mulroy looked askance at Fleagle.

Violet knew Mulroy had a digital recorder on his person. When she'd first listened to the recording, perhaps she'd imagined the look on his face when he spoke those words. Was that the memory she was re-living now? Something she'd *imagined*? "Are you kidding me?" she muttered.

"This was a mistake," Mulroy said bitterly.

Violet turned away. "I don't want to be here for this!" she whimpered. "I don't want to see…"

"I knew you wouldn't believe me," drawled Fleagle. "No one ever does."

Violet closed her eyes, waited five seconds, then opened them again.

She was still in the parking lot. The scene was still playing out. "No!" She tried again. When she opened them this time, she saw Mulroy marching away.

Fleagle's voice called, "Do you wanna know who the girl is or not?"

Mulroy wheeled around and hissed, "Who is she, then?"

Violet looked up into his face. His eyes gleamed with hungry ambition. His mouth curled condescendingly. Everything about him spoke of ruthlessness and contempt. When Violet first met him, he was assaulting a teenage girl—not for the first time, it later transpired. That girl had grown into Violet's best friend.

In a few moments, Cy's molester would be shot through the torso and die alone. Not once had Violet mourned his death. She had no reason to.

Why, then—*why*…did she feel pity for him now?

Fleagle drew a deep breath and spoke with frightening gravity. "The girl with no memory of her past possesses a secret that will shake the town of Veil to its core. It's her destiny to bring down a great evil that's festered here for years. Their showdown is inevitable—" He broke off.

"What? What is it?" Rob snapped. Violet watched as he darted over to Fleagle, who backed away, looking all around in fright.

"Someone followed us! Followed *you!*" Fleagle tried to run. Rob restrained him. "Let me go! They'll kill me!"

Violet looked on and waited. *You don't deserve a witness,* she thought at Rob. Yet she remained and kept her eyes on him.

The gunshot made her jump even though she expected it. The shooter was nowhere in sight. The men were seemingly frozen in shock, then, as Rob slid to the ground, Violet glimpsed him slipping the recorder into Fleagle's jacket pocket.

Fleagle clearly expected to be downed next. He stood there, shaking like a leaf, until it was readily apparent that he was to be spared. "I don't understand!" he cried. "Why him and not me?!" Those were the last words spoken here. In a moment Fleagle would run off in fright, would leave his jacket (and the recorder) in his apartment and then disappear to who knew where.

Except he wasn't running away. He seemed paralyzed. Violet frowned. Why wasn't he running?

Back when Violet was still in the real world, in the moment she realized what Sheriff Dubowski was about to do, it had taken all of her courage to shove at his arm, to try to stop him from shooting Joy, instead of simply fleeing. Never before had she felt such a thrill of horror, like suddenly noticing a hungry, toothy beast just nearby. She never wanted to feel that again.

What she felt when she heard the laughter was far worse.

* * *

Lying in a bed in a hospital recovery room, Violet twitched. On the nearby monitor, her heart rate shot upward for a moment, but not long enough to alert an attendant nurse.

Out in the hallway, someone in a hooded jacket approached the room.

* * *

Tuck Fleagle was gone. Violet was alone with Rob Mulroy's corpse. She wanted to stand back up, but her legs were shaking uncontrollably. Although the laughter had ceased, it still rang inside her head, gleeful, malevolent.

27

She knew she had to get up. Rob's body was not found here in this parking lot, it was found elsewhere, weeks later. That meant that someone—Rob's killer—the person who had laughed that awful laugh—was on their way here.

But they can't see me, part of Violet thought desperately. *I'm not really here. This is just a memory.*

...Isn't it? There had been no laughter on the tape recording.

She heard a noise behind her. Adrenaline shot her to her feet. But it wasn't someone approaching.

It was Rob. He was coughing, struggling for breath.

Violet stared in disbelief. "No...no, this can't be what happened. I'm not psychic. This isn't a memory anymore. This is just a dream."

Rob's eyes were wide open but unseeing. He drew a last, raspy breath. "Cy... I'm sorry..."

His jaw went slack. He was dead.

Violet shook her head emphatically. The motion caused her hair to fall in front of her face. When she brushed it away, she found herself no longer in the parking lot. She was on a footbridge. A corner of the sky glowed with false dawn.

"What the hell??!!"

* * *

The door of Violet's recovery room opened slowly, quietly. Whoever was entering held the doorknob in one hand. The other hand held a hypodermic syringe.

* * *

"You have got to be kidding me!!" Violet roared, having just realized where—and when—she was.

Sure enough, at the end of the bridge there appeared a running figure. Jogging, to be more accurate. Though it was too dark to see, Violet knew exactly who it was: Matt Foley, who, when alive, had been an enemy of Candy's. Like with Rob, Violet had only run into him twice before his demise. The last time had been quite a confrontation. No one was certain when exactly Foley had been murdered—except, of course, his murderer—but it couldn't have been too long after that last—

"But I *wasn't here!*" Violet protested. "How can I have memories of something I didn't see?!" Possibly, when she'd read about the evidence, she'd reconstructed in her head how the killing must have occurred. But this was too *detailed* to be a replica of what she'd pictured. The way Foley slowed his pace as he crossed the bridge, paused at the end, leaned over the rail as he caught his breath, staring into the gently flowing Greene River... She couldn't subconsciously reconstruct his behavior based on knowing him for only a few days back in October!

Could she?

It startled her when the killer, clad in black from head to toe, came up to Foley from behind. Where had he sprung out from? Though she knew it was futile, Violet couldn't help shrieking, *"Look out!!!"*

She almost thought Foley heard her, for he turned his head slightly a moment before the killer struck him in the back with a heavy stick. Violet gasped and backed into the bridge railing. This wasn't the first time she'd seen that behemoth unleashing a barrage of brutality. She knew exactly whose face was beneath that mask: Kurt Riner. The former prosecuting attorney and mayoral candidate had killed at least four people in Veil and several more before that in other towns. Two months ago, Violet had exposed him as the serial killer. Any day now he'd be going to trial.

Matt Foley was an athletic specimen, but he was no match for his larger assailant. Violet flinched at every blow, every crunch of bone. When the last strike caught him on the side of the head and pitched him over the bridge railing, she turned away. She could hear Foley's neck break on impact with the rocks in the shallow water.

Hesitantly, she looked back. Riner was surveying his victim from above. Satisfied Foley was dead, he strode to the end of the bridge and purposefully wedged the stick into the metalwork, where Deputy Benno would discover it on Halloween night. Then he trotted away, whistling the tune of "Pop Goes the Weasel."

Violet did a double take. What was Riner doing? He couldn't have just *left* after killing Foley. He'd preserved the body so as to stage its discovery several days later.

And yet Foley's corpse floated there, in the shallows, undisturbed.

Of course, it didn't matter. None of this was real anyway. It was just a dream.

Except, deep down, Violet knew—*she didn't believe that.*

* * *

Joy had had no objection to sharing a recovery room with Violet. When a nurse brought Joy upstairs for a brief medical test, Joy was concerned for Violet—what if the girl woke up and no one was there to ease her back into consciousness? The nurse assured her Violet would only be alone for a few minutes.

Twenty minutes later, the nurse and Deputy Tan escorted Joy back toward her room. Joy rounded the corner first—and saw someone in a dark jacket with the hood pulled up at the door of the room in which Violet was sleeping. The person was halfway across the threshold.

And holding a needle.

"Hey!" shouted Joy. "What are you doing in there?"

30

The figure darted away and around the corner, and was out of sight by the time the nurse and the deputy caught up with Joy.

* * *

Violet should have seen this coming. "No," she moaned. "No, please, no."

She wasn't on the footbridge anymore. She was in a playground. It was still nighttime.

Halloween night, to be exact.

"No..." Violet saw a black cat strolling through the playground. A person dressed up as a black cat, that is. A young woman, whose name was Marcy Temple.

Marcy would never leave this playground alive. Any moment now, that same masked figure was going to knock her unconscious, then snap her neck. The body would be dragged under the slide, and pepper poured over her face to tie in with a nursery rhyme, the serial killer's signature.

Violet felt her body racking with sobs. She'd watched Rob Mulroy's murder, and Foley's. She had no right to look away from Marcy's. She'd barely known her, yet since her death she'd grieved terribly. It was so wrong, what had happened to her—what was about to happen—

Violet yelped. The masked figure was already approaching, creeping up behind Marcy, only a few feet away. Again, Violet had missed his emergence from his hiding place.

He had something in his hand. He lifted it high, then brought it smashing down. Marcy crumpled in a senseless heap.

Violet's heart pounded in her ears.

The killer sat on Marcy's back, reached around and took hold of her head on opposite sides. In a moment, with one mighty twist, he'd—

"NOOOO!!!" In a fury, Violet charged forward—
And knocked the killer off his victim.

Violet swung and kicked wildly, yowling at the top of her lungs. Surely someone would hear and come to her aid. This seemed to occur to the killer as well, for he sprinted away without a backward glance.

Violet almost whooped with laughter. "I did it!" she cried. "I DID IT!" She sped back to Marcy's side and shook her. "Marcy! Marcy, wake up. You can wake up now, you're okay." Marcy didn't stir. She was hardly breathing.

Violet stared at her. Her excitement faded. She half-sat, half-fell onto the ground beside her.

When she spoke a minute later, it was in a dull monotone. "I could imagine you alive again. But it wouldn't do the real you any good. Probably wouldn't do me any good either, come to think of it." She sighed heavily. "I liked you. A lot. But I hardly knew you. When you died, I had no idea there was a serial killer. I'd barely even started to figure myself out. I wasn't responsible for keeping you safe. What happened to you isn't part of my story, so *why am I so upset?!!"*

She covered her face, weeping. After a moment, she said, more quietly, "If you'd lived, you'd have been kind and loving and inspirational...and happy. You would've been so happy. And you deserved to be. When someone dies an untimely death, people talk about loved ones' loss and survivors' guilt and all the things the person could've done with their life, the success they could've had. But I think we forget—even *I* forget that the biggest loss is...is the life the person would've lived. And I don't mean the things they'd have done, I mean what they would've *experienced.* The moments no one would ever know except them. The stories, the memories, the feelings. *Those* are the precious things that got taken away." Her speech felt faintly petulant, but Violet didn't care. She'd been struggling for these words for ages, and finally she'd found them. "I am so sorry, Marcy. I understand your loss and I grieve for it."

Violet felt a gentle hand take hers.

A soft voice said, "Thank you."

Violet looked up and found Marcy sitting up, facing her. Wordlessly they leaned forward and hugged.

When Violet had enough courage, she whispered, "I'll miss you."

Marcy whispered back, "There are others who can be saved."

Violet drew back with a frown. "What do you mean?"

"You know what I mean."

Violet felt a dreadful chill. "No... We caught him. We caught the serial killer. It was Kurt Riner. He's the killer." But even as she said it, the question came back to her: after killing Foley, why did Riner leave the body in the river when the killer *must* have collected it? Unless...

"Unless *there's more than one.*"

IV

Since the death of her predecessor, none of Sheriff Grogan's deputies had called her by her new title. She didn't blame them, though as she approached the hospital entrance, she wondered which of them would eventually be the first to overcome their discomfort and—

"Sheriff Grogan!"

Jen turned and found not one of her deputies, but a sandy-haired man in his thirties running up to her. "Chuck? What are you doing here?"

"*Veil Chronicle.*"

Jen gave him a blank stare. "What about it?"

"It—they—I'm with them. I'm with the *Chronicle.* May I ask you a few questions?"

Chuck Benz—a reporter? When did that happen? "Sorry, Chuck, I'm really busy right now."

"Okay, well, off the record, is Violet okay? Is she awake?" Chuck seemed more concerned than put off.

"I don't know," said Jen. As she entered the building, she added under her breath, "If not, then she's about to be."

But the hospital staff told her, unequivocally, that would not happen. For the sake of her health and recovery, Violet's body had to be allowed to decide when she should wake up. It might happen today...or it might not.

Sheriff Grogan told the hospital staff and Deputy Derrick that she needed to know the *minute* Violet was conscious. Unfortunately, one of those parties had to be told the exact reason.

The officers were allowed the use of an empty office. Derrick stared out the window with an expression of stupefaction. "There's got to be an explanation," he said hoarsely, "a reason why he had Bethany Williams's phone."

"There is," Grogan said matter-of-factly. "Keith Dubowski, our friend and leader, abducted and attempted to rape Bethany. When he found out about our plan to trap the perp, he decided to use it to frame Felix Bancourt. He didn't know at the time about Micah Rourke sneaking into Bethany's room while she was away, or he might've chosen a different scapegoat. Felix had attacked Bethany verbally and publicly, so he seemed like the logical choice. Dubowski was lying when he told me about having a flat tire last night; he must've given it a flat, himself, to back up his story. He sent Felix that text from Bethany's phone, which he'd stolen when he kidnapped her. He parked on Dime Road and waited for Felix to show up so he could take him down and play the hero. I have no idea how, but somehow Violet figured out that Dubowski was the culprit. She confronted him..." Grogan frowned. "No. No, she wouldn't have done that. She would've come to me. Joy said she had a look on her face. What if Violet figured it out right then, standing behind him in line? Dubowski sees her horrified expression, and he realizes she knows the truth. He has to silence her. But Joy's there, too. Violet's right next to him, but Joy's farther away. She might escape. So he takes her out first..."

"It was Pressler," Derrick blurted out.

"What?"

"The sheriff thought Pressler was out to kill him. He, he had to be on his guard all the time. It must've... It must've made him... He, he wasn't himself. He would never have done those things if—"

"If making excuses for him is your way of dealing with this, then you're going to have to do it alone."

"Look, it might be easy for you, but—"

"*Easy?!*" Grogan advanced on him. "My job is to protect this town and also to make people feel safe. They're completely different tasks. Don't think for a *second* that my seeming calm and collected means I'm not freaking out over this as much as you are! He was my mentor, too! We both looked up to him since we were kids!"

Sullen-faced, Derrick asked, "What are you going to tell people?"

"I can't tell them anything until Violet wakes up and confirms what the evidence is saying. *Then* I'll figure out what to—Cy!"

Cy stood awkwardly in the office doorway. "I—tried knocking."

"Cy, where have you been?" her mother demanded. "I've been calling you!"

Cy cleared her throat. "Mom, I need to—" To her surprise, Jen suddenly hugged her.

"I'm sorry," Jen murmured. She kissed the top of Cy's head. "I'm sorry, I was just worried about you."

After a moment Cy hugged her mother back, at first half-heartedly, then much more tightly.

"Come on," said Jen. "I'll take you to Violet."

Cy hesitated a little, then followed.

Deputy Tan sat in a chair outside the recovery room. When Tan saw Grogan approaching, she seemed about to say something, then reconsidered when she saw Cy.

They opened the door in time to hear someone saying, "I never even thought to ask—" Candy saw them entering and fell silent. She was sitting beside Violet, holding her hand.

Cy gasped at the sight of her friend in the bed. A gauzy bandage covered her head. Her face and neck were purple with bruises. She looked nothing like herself.

As Cy went to Candy and hugged her, across the room, Joy sat up in her bed. "Jen! Did you find him?"

Deputy Derrick groaned. Grogan looked from him to Joy. "Find whom?"

Joy stared at Derrick in disbelief. "You didn't tell her?!"

Grogan fixed her deputy with a steely glare. "Tell me what?"

Before Derrick could say anything, Joy fairly shouted, "I saw someone—not a nurse or doctor—trying to come in here while Violet was alone."

Sighing, Derrick said, "It was probably just someone who had the wrong door."

"They had a *needle!* They were after Violet, I know it!"

Both Cy and Candy turned to Grogan in alarm. "Did anyone else see this person?" asked the sheriff.

"No," said Derrick.

"Um," said a small voice. Everyone turned to Deputy Tan, standing just inside the door. "Sheriff Grogan, may I speak to you?" She indicated the hallway with a head gesture.

Closing the door behind them, Tan reported, "One of the nurses just told me they found a back entrance open that shouldn't be. The staff is keeping watch for someone unauthorized to be here, but—"

Derrick interrupted her, "Are we really treating this seriously? Who would be trying to hurt Violet?"

"Hm," Grogan said mildly. "Off the top of my head: Mayor Pressler's old assistant, Ernie; Pressler, himself; one of those three thieves from Halloween; anyone from the group Wholesome; the Lammwych family…"

"Her girlfriend's ex," put in Tan.

"Oh, and the woman who kidnapped her and my daughter a few weeks ago. Just to name a few."

Derrick scowled. "Well, what can we do? We already have a deputy watching the door."

Jen took a moment to consider. Then she went back into the room and said, "Cy, I need to borrow your jacket."

* * *

"Mmmmeeep."

Violet went still for a moment, processing her new location. She was indoors now. It was dark, but there was no mistaking that familiar sound. She was at home—the Grogan home—and the hand that a moment ago had been holding Marcy's now stroked the cat, Roswell. She was sitting on the floor beside him. "Mmeep," he repeated, then, as if on a whim, rose to his feet, trotted across the floor, and leapt onto the banister beside the stairs that faced the front door.

Part of Violet wondered why she was here, but at the forefront of her mind was a more pressing question: could there really be two serial killers? Had Kurt Riner been working with someone all along? Was that a thing, serial killers working together? Could Riner *really* have had a helper?

Unless he *was the helper…*

Violet thought back to the night she'd unmasked him. Several minor things had to her seemed unresolved at the time, but one thing now stood out. All that night, between the murders of Amy Chester and Byron Temple, and the abduction of Trisha Sinclair, and Violet's own eventual capture, a sinister voice had taunted Violet over the phone—a phone that had been left for her to find. First, the disguised voice made her believe the killer knew her true identity, then it professed to have a personal connection with her. When Violet demanded to know why he was killing all these people, the voice spoke of a promise to be kept, but wouldn't say exactly what that promise was.

Violet had chosen to believe that everything the voice had told her was a lie, though one definite impression she'd formed was that the killer was at least *interested* in her, perhaps even *wanted* to tell her his secrets. But when Kurt Riner held her hostage in that abandoned building, he'd shown no such interest at all.

If it hadn't been Kurt's voice on the phone, then whose was it?

Over on the banister, Roswell's body suddenly tensed. In a moment, Violet saw why: the front door was rattling. Someone was trying to get in, picking the lock. All at once, Violet knew what day it was: this was the day before Kurt Riner was unmasked. At this point in time, Violet had been on a camping trip with the Grogans and Trisha. While they'd been away, the killer had broken in and left the cellular phone on Violet's bed. This must be when the killer entered and—

The door opened and Elijah Pressler came inside.

"Pressler?!" Violet said aloud, though he couldn't hear her. This didn't make any sense. Pressler was far from an innocent man, but—the serial killer? Surely not.

Violet thought back to the last conversation they'd had. It had been earlier today (assuming it still *was* today in the real world). Pressler had informed her that what was "about to happen" was her fault, for interfering in his (criminal) affairs. What exactly had he meant?

Had Pressler somehow *arranged* for the sheriff to try to kill her??!

No, that was absurd. Discovering the sheriff's guilty secret had been a complete accident, Violet was sure. Whatever threat Pressler had intended to carry out, it must've been planned for later.

Violet followed the mayor—or mayor-to-be, at this point in time—through the house, watched as he searched her bedroom. She was already aware that he'd gone through her things, but seeing it firsthand made her doubly nauseated.

"Seriously?" she growled as Pressler reached under her mattress and pulled out the calendar Cy had given her. Photos of attractive, partially clothed women accompanied each month.

When Pressler flipped through the pages, Violet glimpsed the model above the month of April. Two months ago, when Violet blacked out during a fight, she'd found herself in what appeared to be a therapist's office. The therapist who had spoken to her was named April, and it had taken Violet an eternity to remember that it was the same "April" from the calendar—in appearance at least. *Who was she?* Violet wondered again.

But what she wondered more was what she was doing here. This incident had nothing to do with the serial killer, so why had she been brought here? She glanced about, out the window, into the hall—and did a double take.

Roswell had sped out of the room a moment ago. Violet had thought he'd run all the way down the hall, but he'd halted just outside the door, ears flattened back, eyes fixed on something.

Violet joined him. She saw nothing unusual ahead of them, just the hallway, the far window facing the front of the house, and the main staircase, leading down to the front door. Still the cat's attention was fixated in that direction. Violet crept down the hall and stopped at the top of the stairs. Her stomach did a somersault.

Pressler had closed the front door behind him, *but now it was ajar.*

The killer was here. Pressler and the serial killer had intruded into the house at the same time!

Violet heard a voice and glanced back. Pressler was talking to himself. She looked forward again—and jumped. *The killer was standing at the bottom of the stairs, looking up at her.*

Except he couldn't see her, could he? He was just a memory—for she'd accepted that's what this was, even if she couldn't explain it.

As the killer silently mounted the stairs, Violet pressed herself against the wall. He passed by her without a glance. As before, his face was hidden beneath a black woolen mask covering his whole head—a balaclava, with tiny holes for the eyes and mouth. There wasn't even a hint of the killer's face. The person was taller than Violet, but then that hardly narrowed it down.

The killer slipped into Jen's bedroom and hid there just as Pressler reappeared in the hall. Heading downstairs, he seemed to be in some kind of daze. The killer's head peeked out from the bedroom. Pressler had no idea he was being watched.

Then again, the same could be said of the killer. Violet approached him hesitantly, her heart pounding. *He's not real,* she told herself. *He can't hurt me.*

But wouldn't he react to her if she touched him, as he had before? How badly could he hurt her in this dreamscape?

Could he kill her?

Taking a deep breath, she stretched out her hand.

Pressler stepped outside and turned to close the door.

Violet's fingers were inches from the mask when the killer withdrew his head, vanishing into the darkened room. She'd hesitated too long.

Pressler was re-locking the door from outside. Violet waited for the killer to re-emerge once Pressler was gone. *I'll just rip off the mask and then run like hell,* she said to herself, watching the door below.

"Mmmeep," came Roswell's voice from behind her. Violet turned—

She barely had time to shriek before the killer's fist slammed into her chest. She collided with the wall, tripped and fell over. The killer bore down on her like a bird of prey. With frantic cries, Violet skittered backward, crab-like. Her cry became a scream when her hand found empty space behind her. She was back at the top of the stairs. Grabbing the banister post, she heaved herself to her feet.

The killer lifted a leg to deliver a mighty kick. In the instant before impact, Violet shrieked: *"APRIL!!!"*

Next moment, she flew backward through the air...

And landed on a soft sofa. Shaken, she looked all around. She was in an office. A therapist's office.

"Well," said a familiar voice.

Trembling, Violet turned to see April standing behind the sofa, dunking a tea bag into a steaming ceramic mug. She sipped from it tenderly.

"Took you long enough."

V

A nurse wheeled a gurney down the hall to the recovery room occupied by Violet. As she brought the gurney inside, her voice could be heard from the hallway: "I just need to take Violet upstairs for some tests. It won't take long."

"Can I go with her?" came Candy's voice.

"Candy, you haven't eaten since you got here," said the voice of the sheriff. "You're starting to look pale. You should get something to eat."

"I'll stay with Violet," Cy volunteered.

A moment later Candy left the room and headed toward the cafeteria.

"Joy, we have some follow-up questions for you, when you're ready." This was followed by a steady drone from Deputy Derrick.

After a minute, the nurse came out with Violet on the gurney, Cy trailing along in her cyan jacket with the hood pulled up. They went into an elevator, got out on a floor where there weren't as many people about, and brought the gurney to an examination room. Five minutes later, Cy went down the hall to a restroom.

The person who'd been spying on them crept out of the

43

stairwell and cracked open the examination room door. The nurse was nowhere in sight. Violet was alone in the darkened room.

The person eased open the door and tiptoed toward Violet—who suddenly sat up and held up a hand. "Hold it!" She reached up and tore off the bandage. It wasn't Violet on the gurney, but Sheriff Grogan.

The person doubled back but found his way blocked by the woman in the cyan jacket. She pulled down the hood, revealing Deputy Tan.

"Tan, the lights," ordered the sheriff.

The man seemed to take his capture in stride. With a sigh of resignation, he turned back toward Grogan.

She straightened up in surprise. "Well, well. Tuck Fleagle."

* * *

Under normal circumstances, Sheriff Grogan would've immediately taken Fleagle to the station. Deep down, she knew she should. But she couldn't bring herself to leave the hospital just yet, not with Violet still asleep. A rational part of her argued that whether or not Violet would wake up had nothing to do with Jen's presence or absence, but she paid no attention.

Thus she found herself once again in the unoccupied office, utilizing it as a makeshift interrogation room. Fleagle sat behind the empty desk. Deputy Tan stood at the door, arms crossed.

"I wasn't trying to—hurt the girl," Fleagle insisted. "I was—afraid for her." He spoke haltingly, as if he had difficulty recalling certain words. His skin was a sickly color, his hair a tangled mess. His shoddy clothes gave off a strong odor.

Grogan remembered Fleagle was an alcoholic, but he didn't seem drunk now. Under-slept and badly in need of hygiene, but not drunk. "You snuck into the hospital," she began.

"To make sure she was all right." He nodded several times.

"What was the needle for, then?"

Fleagle blinked hard. "Needle? What needle?"

"You were seen outside Violet's room holding a needle."

"That wasn't me! That must've been..." A shudder rippled through Fleagle. His hands went back and forth indecisively between his chin and the desk. "Oh my god," he murmured. "Oh my god, they're here. Here in Veil. Here in the hospital."

"Who's here?"

Fleagle looked up, as if he'd forgotten she was listening. He uttered a dry, humorless laugh. "I could tell you," he rasped. "Just like I've told it again and again, over and over. No one ever listens more than once. No one ever believes me."

"Mr. Fleagle, right now you're looking at an attempted murder charge, so if I were you, I'd try very hard to be believable."

He snorted and gave her a belligerent stare. Grogan calmly stared back and waited. Finally, he blew out his breath. "Fine. But before I tell you, you should know something." He lowered his voice, which took on a conspiratorial quality. "The last person to whom I tried to impart this secret was killed right in front of me. Shot from a distance." He leaned toward her. "That person...was Rob Mulroy, from the *Chronicle*."

The sheriff scrutinized him. Her gut told her he was in earnest; he wasn't trying to play mind games. He really thought he was telling her something she didn't already know. Which led to an intriguing paradox. Since he disappeared last October, he'd apparently been living far enough off the grid not to have learned of the developments in the Mulroy investigation, yet somehow he'd heard that Violet had been brought to the hospital.

"I know you all think Mulroy was just another of the serial killer's victims," Fleagle was saying, "but someone else killed him. In fact," he added, more to himself than to her, "it's possible there might not even really *be* a serial killer."

Grogan pulled him back on track. "If someone didn't want you giving away a secret, why didn't they kill you along with Mulroy? Why let you live?"

"I wondered that, myself," breathed Fleagle. "It must be because they still have plans for me. Just like they have plans for her."

"For Violet, you mean?"

"Violet," Fleagle repeated musingly. "Before I went into hiding, you were calling her Nelly."

It was Grogan's turn to lean forward. "Do you know her real name? Her real identity?"

A cagey look appeared in Fleagle's eyes. He closed them briefly and drew a breath through his nose, as if steeling himself. "How long have you lived in Veil, Sheriff?"

Grogan's eyebrow twitched. "I moved back here last August."

"You'd lived here before?"

"I was born here. I left almost fifteen years ago."

Fleagle tilted his head to the side and paused. "In that case… there's a chance that *you* know who Violet really is."

Grogan gave him a quizzical frown.

Fleagle shrugged. "You've just forgotten."

* * *

Violet jumped to her feet and faced April with the sofa between them. Her heart was still pounding, or so it felt in this dreamscape. When she'd called out April's name, she hadn't been sure what to expect. She only knew that the last time she'd gone head-to-head with the serial killer (or one of them), she'd have lost if not for April. Violet wasn't sure if calling for April had caused April to appear, or if—and this had disturbing implications—April had heard Violet and *brought her here.*

April held up the ceramic mug. "Would you like some tea?" When Violet didn't answer, April gave her a weak smile, with something in her eyes that looked like fondness. "It really is good to see you again."

Violet swallowed. "What are you?"

April didn't seem at all offended by Violet's choice of "what" over "who." If anything, she looked impressed. "What do you think I am?"

"I have no clue. Are you...my conscience?"

April smirked in amusement.

"My...subconscious mind?"

"Nope."

"Alternate personality?"

April hooted with laughter. "Very much no." She glanced down at her figure. "If that were the case, I'd say you have some vanity issues."

Violet stared hard at her. She chanced a step closer. "Are you—me? Me from before I lost my memories?"

April sobered instantly. "No. I'm sorry."

Violet shook her head impatiently. "I just need to know if you're the one doing this."

"Doing what?"

"Taking me down this—this nightmare memory lane. Only they're not all memories! Except—they are?"

April held out the mug of tea. "You're in control of your own mind, Violet."

After a moment, Violet accepted the tea. It was warm and soothing, though curiously flavorless.

"But it's true," said April. "The things you've seen are more than memories. If you like, you could call them Truths."

Violet regarded her warily over the rim of the mug. "I don't believe in psychic visions."

"Well, it depends on whether you define 'psychic' as the cause or the result."

Violet's reply was deadpan. "What?"

April rounded the sofa. "Ordinarily you can't see things that are behind you. But if you look in a mirror, you can. Why is that?"

"Because of the reflection."

"Exactly. But not all reflections are visible. And not everyone sees the world the same way. Sometimes there are reflections seen by a few people, but not the rest. You could say those few see more than others because they're psychic, or you could say they're psychic because they see more than others."

Violet took another gulp of tea before trying to reason this out. "Are you saying that something about my brain...makes me...*like* a psychic?"

April smiled. "You see? You're much better at explaining it than I am. You don't even need me."

"But..." Violet shook her head and sank onto the sofa. "It just doesn't make sense. What 'reflections' could I be seeing?"

April sat next to her. "I look at it this way. When people watch the rain, they see rain. When they look at a campfire, they see fire. But if you asked them to describe the *shape* of the rain, the *shape* of the fire, they couldn't tell you."

"I couldn't tell you, either," Violet said wryly.

April looked at her steadily.

After a moment Violet went on, staring off to the side, "But you're right. I, I know exactly what you mean when you say...

But I don't know the words to describe…"

"No one would understand you no matter what words you chose. You mustn't blame yourself for not being able to find something that doesn't exist."

"But I can't even describe it to myself! I could say there are patterns I recognize, but it's more than that. There just isn't any…"

"Context."

Violet looked at April and saw her wearing a strange expression. It seemed to be pride mixed with sympathy. Perhaps April was simply part of Violet who understood her better than the rest of her did.

Hesitantly Violet reached over and touched April's hand. "Thank you," she said. "For saving me the last time we met."

"You saved yourself," April replied. "I just helped."

"Can you help me again? I mean, if I'm stuck in my own head, I might as well try."

"Try what?"

"To find out who the serial killer is."

Though her expression didn't change, April paled.

"Is that something I can do? Is that a 'Truth' I can uncover?"

April nodded slowly. "People have shapes, too."

"I get the feeling you're not talking about silhouettes."

"What am I talking about?"

Violet thought for a moment. "Personalities. Behavior. Choices."

April raised her eyebrows encouragingly.

"Um…minds?"

April wrinkled her nose. "'Mind' is a vague term, a place-holder for things we don't understand yet—though it makes us feel as if we already do."

Violet thought about the people she'd met in Veil. Although she had no idea what the exact population was, she knew the precise number of those she'd seen with her own eyes. There were others she'd only heard of, but those she'd seen, even if only for a split second, she could recognize in a heartbeat.

But there was a deeper recognition, which grew stronger for the people she'd spent more time around. Something— again—that couldn't be described in words, only feelings. It was this that gave Violet a view of the happiness Marcy Temple would have had in living out her life. It was this that made Violet sure that Rob Mulroy had repented for his sins in the moments before his death, even though in life he'd never shown any evidence of remorse. Violet was able to see something in them that no one else could—their *shapes*... Their...

"Souls." Violet nearly dropped the mug. "I can—recognize souls. I can recognize them by the actions they take."

April nodded, beaming. "And vice versa. Because they're one and the same."

Violet frowned. "But then why didn't it work? When I tried to unmask the killer, I barely got close enough. Did I do something wrong?"

April looked down uncomfortably. "I'd say...it's because you haven't fully committed."

"Not committed?! Of course I'm committed! I want to stop him before he kills more people!"

April looked her in the eye. "But there was something else you wanted to do, wasn't there?"

"Something else??" And then Violet realized... "I tried to remember who I am. Who I was before my memory loss."

April heaved a deep sigh. "You could."

Violet's eyes nearly popped out. "I could?!"

"You could get all your memories back. Reclaim your past, your full identity."

Violet was speechless with jubilation.

"Or you could unmask the killer."

Violet felt her spirits plummet. "'*Or*'?"

"Your gift is strong, but like everything else, it has its limits."

"Are you saying I have to choose? Between my memories and...?"

April chewed her tongue for a moment, apparently giving serious thought to her response. Then— "Have some more tea."

VI

Cy was dozing off at Violet's bedside when she felt something being draped around her shoulders. It was her jacket.

"Have you had anything to eat since you got here?" asked her mother.

Cy nodded, blinking herself awake. The only other person in the room was Joy, fast asleep. "Where's Candy?"

"I sent her home—for real this time. We'll call her if Violet wakes up. *When* she wakes up."

Violet's wounds were still difficult to look at. Cy almost wished Violet could sleep through the healing process and wake up after the pain was all over.

Jen patted Cy on the shoulder. "Come on."

As Cy stood up, she looked at the clock and saw how late it was. "Are you sending me home, too?"

"I don't think so."

"Wait, really? Why not?"

Jen glanced at Violet, and in that glance Cy caught sight of how worried she really was. "Because I don't want you alone right now," Jen said.

They passed Deputy Derrick outside the door, standing guard.

Derrick closed the door after them and stood at attention, seemingly oblivious to the chair on his other side.

"Where are we going, then?" Cy asked her mother.

"Well, Tuck Fleagle is still in the office we're using, so we can sit here." Jen led Cy down a quiet hallway to a pair of cushioned, armless chairs. "And we can discuss whatever it is you're anxious to talk to me about."

"Oh." Startled just as she was sitting down, Cy froze in mid-motion, then sat down the rest of the way.

Jen regarded her expectantly.

"Um…what about Fleagle? Did he tell you anything?"

"My deputies are checking on his story." Jen grunted to herself. "*My* deputies."

"Was it really him outside Violet's room earlier, with the needle in his hand? Did he say anything about her? I mean, you guys have been trying to track him down for months, to see if he really knows Violet's true identity."

Jen nodded and said casually, "He did tell us her identity, generally speaking."

Cy's jaw dropped.

"Though personally I find it hard to swallow. But—" She looked her daughter in the eye. "I can tell that's not what's really on your mind."

Cy looked down, her cheeks reddening.

Gently Jen said, "Cy, now that I'm the sheriff, things are going to be different. It's going to take some getting used to. It'll be harder for us to talk together right when we need to. That means we're both going to have to seize moments like these. Do you understand?"

Cy nodded, still not looking at her. "Yeah, I, um…"

Jen gave her arm an affectionate squeeze. "Take your time."

Cy took a deep breath. Then another. "I—Luther and I broke up."

Jen sat up straight. Her voice stayed calm, but her eyes bespoke rage. "What did he do?"

"No, no, no, I mean—*he* broke up with *me*."

Jen blinked hard. For a moment she was at a loss, then: "I'll kill him."

A chuckle burst out of Cy, then she said in a low voice, "Mom, you're the sheriff now. You can't say that."

"True," said Jen. There was a pause. "I'll still kill him."

They looked at each other. Jen smiled.

"Mom, I know about the abortion."

Jen gave a little gasp. On her face was a look of astonishment.

"I mean, I know you tried to have an abortion when you were pregnant with me, and you weren't allowed to."

Astonishment turned to befuddlement.

"But it's okay," Cy rushed on, "because I'm not mad. I mean, I was when I first found out, but now I—I mean, whatever was going on, it was your choice, your right to decide about your own body. I can't judge you and still be pro-choice—except I don't judge you anyway, because—because of what I said. And I'm not sure how I feel about it, but it—it doesn't change how I feel about *you*. I love you, and I know you love me. I don't know if us talking about it will help—"

"Cy!" Jen took hold of her hands. "Cy...honey, I didn't *try* to have an abortion. I *did* have an abortion."

Cy was thunderstruck. "Wh-what?"

Jen let go of her hands and heaved a deep sigh. When she spoke, she sounded distant, as if these things had happened to someone else. "It was almost two years after Azura was born. I was still married to her father. We were expecting

54

our second baby. But then we found out I...I had a clotting disorder." Flashes of emotion appeared on her face. Her effort to remain calm became more pronounced.

Cy took her hand.

Jen swallowed. "I wanted to have the baby, but if I'd carried to term, then most likely we both would've died." She looked at Cy. Her voice began to choke as she said, "I hope you never have to make a decision like that."

"Mom, I had no idea."

Jen sighed. "I think I've gotten into a bad habit of not talking about painful memories. It's something I need to work on."

"Was this the reason you and Cliff split up?"

"Hm? Oh, no, that was... No."

"Does Azura know?"

"I think her father told her." Jen shook her head slowly. "I thought, at the time...I wouldn't be able to have any more kids." She turned to Cy, her eyes shining with tears, and smiled. "But then I had you. A miracle that came out of the blue. So I named you Cyanne."

Cy's heart was breaking. Just this morning she'd decided, in a heartbeat, to leave this person forever, based on what should have been an obvious lie. She wanted to dash from the hospital, tear back to Myrna's house, rush her belongings back home, and shred the note she'd left for her mother. The very thought of hurting this woman made her sick.

"Mom, I am so sorry," she said hoarsely. "I'm so sorry."

Cy knew she'd eventually have to explain how she got the terrible idea into her head in the first place, so it surprised her when, instead of asking, Jen said, "You know, you've seemed really happy since the new year. I love to see you happy, but honestly I expected a lot more angst and cynicism." She touched

Cy's cheek. "Finding out what your father did... I'd understand if you looked at the world and wondered when another shoe is going to drop. Or in this case, when another parent is going to hurt you."

"No!" Cy shook her head vehemently, her own tears starting to make themselves felt. "I'm not gonna live like that. Sometimes people I trust are gonna hurt me, that's just life, but I refuse to let that destroy my faith in the ones who matter the most to me—you, Azura, Uncle Red, Violet—"

She looked up suddenly, her eyes wide with shock. "Oh my god... When Violet came to live with us, and she couldn't remember her real name, and I gave her the name, Violet..."

Jen covered her jaw as her bottom lip started to tremble.

"And then you told me about your friend, Violet, who died when you were a kid..."

Jen lowered her hand and managed to nod. She gave Cy a tremulous smile.

"Violet...was the name you were going to give to the baby, after your friend. That's why you were so upset when I—"

At that moment the dam burst, the emotion too great for Jen to keep contained. She covered her face, shaking with sobs. Cy hugged her fiercely. "I'm here, Mom," she whispered. "I'm here."

* * *

The mug was empty. Violet had drunk all of the tea.

She looked up miserably at April. "Why aren't you telling me I'm being selfish?"

"You've helped a lot of people in Veil. You deserve some answers."

"But I can only get answers by turning my back on those people." She groaned, digging her fingers into her hair. She knew what decision she should make, but letting go of the other option wasn't easy. She might never get another chance to learn her identity.

She reflected on that thought, and she realized it wasn't her memories she was desperate to recover but simply her past. Just to know who she was would be enough, to discover her roots, with or without remembering her time, her experiences as that person. It was horrible, wondering, day after day, if the rest of her life would be spent doing just that—wondering—and now she had the chance to put an end to it…

"It's too bad *you* don't know who I am," she said glumly. "You could just tell me, and then I wouldn't have to choose."

April was silent.

After a moment, Violet noticed what a loud silence it was. She looked up. April's face was neutral. Deliberately, fixedly neutral.

"Oh my god. You—you *do* know who I am."

April's lips parted in trepidation.

Violet raised her voice. "Why haven't you told me??"

"It's—not that simple."

Violet's eyes bugged out. In growing outrage, she stood and pointed down at April's face. "I want you to tell me right now. If you're really part of me, and I'm really in control of my own mind, then I—I order you to tell me!"

April stared up at her. The look in her eyes was something akin to heartbreak. "I can't."

"Then how can I trust you?!"

April said crisply, "I don't know. But you have to."

Violet shook her head, fed up. "No, I don't. Screw it—I'm getting my memories back! I've waited *three whole months.* I've had enough of—"

"Of what?" April stood up. "Being treated with kindness?

Given a home? Forging deep, lasting friendships? Getting multiple chances to do good in the world? Finding a soulmate?"

"That's not fair," spat Violet, shaking with guilt and anger mixed together. "Just a minute ago you said I deserve to remember!"

"That was a different context!"

"Then what are you saying? That my past and my identity are the price I have to pay to have a good life?"

"Is it really that high a price?!"

"It is to me!!" Violet turned away resentfully and headed for the door. Curiously she'd never noticed a door in this room before. Nor, come to think of it, had she noticed that there were no windows.

Her hand was on the doorknob when she heard: "You won't remember."

Violet turned back and said icily, "What?"

"This is a dream." April stepped away from the sofa. "When you wake up, you won't remember any of it."

A long pause followed, filled by an intense battle of stares.

"You're lying," snarled Violet.

April shook her head stolidly.

Violet found herself believing her. She gave an aggravated sigh. "Then it doesn't even matter what I choose!"

April blinked slowly. "There's one way you might remember."

Violet gazed at her acidly. With heavy sarcasm she asked, "Are you going to tell me what it is?"

"If you want me to."

Violet understood the subtext: April was willing to share the information, but she still wanted Violet's trust. "No," said Violet. "No, that doesn't make sense. If what you're saying is true, then there's no reason not to tell me who I am! Not if I'd just forget it anyway—unless…" She half-turned away, her mind racing. "Unless it's something so crucial, I'd *have* to remember it rather than the killer's identity. But what could that—"

"No!" April waved her hands, then put one to her forehead. "No, that's not it at all."

"Then why won't you tell me?!"

"Because you didn't want me to!!" Her breath caught. She stammered, "I, I mean you wouldn't. You wouldn't want me to."

But Violet was staring at her with dawning comprehension. Speaking slowly, she put it together. "We've met before. Before you pretended to be my therapist. When I lost my memories, I must've blacked out. Just before they went, I must've spoken to you. And I made you promise…" In a low, stern tone, she asked, *"Why would I do that?"*

April shrugged in helpless dismay. "I can't tell you."

Violet closed her eyes, took deep breaths. When she had enough control over herself to sound calm, she said, "Fine. How do I remember? Whatever choice I make, how do I keep the information in my memory when I wake up?"

"Well…" April paused, as if considering how to word her answer. She paused for quite some time, her eyes apparently fixed on a spot across the room.

Violet frowned. "April?" She waved a hand in front of her eyes. April didn't react. It was as if she were completely lost in thought.

Then April made a sound. A low, gurgling sound. And *blood dribbled from her mouth—*

Violet let out a cry of horror and recoiled.

A dark shape rose up behind April, who collapsed to the ground. The killer raised a bloody knife and started toward Violet.

VII

Fleagle sat at the hospital office desk, hungrily snacking on a raspberry yogurt.

A piece of paper slid across the desk toward him, then was pulled back. He looked up to see Sheriff Grogan standing on the other side. Her face was flushed, as if she'd been crying. "Finish the yogurt," she ordered. Once he obeyed, she pushed forward a black-and-white image of an elderly woman. "Do you recognize her?"

Fleagle shook his head.

"That's Sharon Brisbon."

Fleagle looked up sharply. "The most recent victim?"

"Her death has been ruled as accidental."

"But you have doubts about that, don't you," Fleagle said shrewdly. "Otherwise why show me her photograph?"

"That isn't a photograph."

Taken aback, Fleagle gave the image a closer look. To his astonishment, he discerned that the lifelike image was pencil-drawn. "This was done by her," he breathed. "By Violet. But why show it to me?"

"As evidence."

"Of what?"

Grogan sat down across from him. "That I gave you the full

benefit of the doubt." She tapped the drawing. "Violet never actually met her. Sharon's obituary contained an old photo, and Violet realized she'd seen her once, weeks before, just outside her house. It was dark, in the early morning, when Violet rode by on her bike. *She drew this from that memory.*" Jen shook her head. "That's just one of the many incredible things I've seen her do. Compared to the theories and scenarios I've run through my head, yours didn't sound half so unlikely."

Fleagle slouched in his chair, his expression halfway between smug and bitter. "So you don't believe me. What a surprise."

"As I said, I gave you the benefit of the doubt. I owe Violet nothing less."

"And I suppose you think it was me who went after her with a needle."

"I go by the evidence, Mr. Fleagle. You told us that just over fifteen years ago, a team of scientists working for a secret branch of the military began experimenting on the citizens of Veil without their knowledge. Their goal was to improve the 'human capacity for memory.'" Grogan spoke without a trace of irony, a fact Fleagle seemed to note grudgingly. "Their efforts were unsuccessful except in the case of one young girl. The scientists kidnapped that girl and wiped her from everyone's memories so that they could continue their experiments on her separately from those still in Veil. Have I got it straight so far?"

Fleagle grunted assent.

"Your memory of all these events has gradually come back to you over the years, but every time you spoke up about it, no one believed you."

"He did," Fleagle interrupted.

"Who?"

"That Mulroy kid. But I've been thinking about it, and I don't think that's why they killed him. I think something went wrong with their experiments, and they had to destroy one of the sample groups. Matt Foley, the Temples, Amy Chester, Sharon Brisbon—they were all part of that group. The whole theory about a serial killer going by the 'Pop Goes the Weasel' song, that's just a cover." He leaned forward suddenly. "What's the story on the sheriff?"

"Excuse me?"

"All I heard on my camp radio was that he died in a shooting, and Violet was seriously injured. That's why I came out of hiding, to check on her. So who's your suspect?"

Grogan thought over her response carefully. "The store proprietor has given a statement that she killed Dubowski in self-defense."

Fleagle shook his head darkly. "Oh, that's bad. They must've altered her memory."

"I thought you said they only have the power to *suppress* memory, like they did to Violet just before she escaped from them."

"No, I said they suppressed her memories *because* she escaped! It's like a fail-safe, or a post-hypnotic suggestion. And it's perfectly possible to alter memories through selective suppression!"

"What about creating memories?"

"What?"

"Do the scientists have the power to *create* new memories as well as suppress them?" Grogan's tone was still conversational, without any sarcasm.

"What are you talking about?"

"As far as the secret military experiments, there wasn't much we could do to check on your story. But we were able to check on *you*. Tuck, you speak a lot about people not believing your conspiracy theories. How you've received so much scorn you're not bothered by it anymore. How you have a reputation as a crackpot. Since you turned up tonight, we spoke to dozens of people from your life: your neighbors, your colleagues at the radio station—we even woke up the man who was sheriff before Dubowski. Know how many of them complained about having to listen to your theories? *None*. Not one of them remembers you saying anything about secret military—"

"Well, there you go! Memory suppression!"

"No, Tuck. *You* created your own reputation. All the stories and rumors about you originated from you, yourself."

"Wrong! I'm *always* spouting conspiracy theories, they just can't remember!"

"Tuck...they also don't remember you from prior to ten years ago."

This threw Fleagle for a moment, then he resumed: "Again—"

"But we did find someone who knows you from before that. Lots of someones, in fact." As if from thin air, Grogan produced a folder and laid it before him. It was filled with photocopies and printouts.

Fleagle opened the folder and found himself staring at a photo of a baby labeled, "Little Tucker." He gave Grogan a suspicious glance. "How could your deputies have put all this together in just a few hours?"

Slowly she replied, "Apparently our way of dealing with the situation with Dubowski is to keep busy. The point is, Tuck, I don't think you lived in Veil your whole life, as you claim. This evidence shows you were born in Connecticut, spent a while in Manhattan, and even—"

"I'm not lying!" snapped Fleagle. He held up the documents.

"These are the lies!"

After a pause, Grogan said, "I don't think you're lying, Tuck. I think, based on this evidence…you're afraid. You're afraid because, for some reason, you can't remember anything of your life from before ten years ago. Maybe you're afraid of finding out you have a medical problem or a psychological disorder. Believe me, I understand that fear. Your reaction, apparently, was to invent a problem that's far worse…but less frightening."

Fleagle shook his head, his certainty wavering. "No, this—this is them. They're—they're covering up—"

"Tuck, my people are here for you if you want to explore your past. They'll stay with you as long as you like. If it turns out someone is lying, trying to hurt you, we'll keep you safe."

Fleagle sat, frowning to himself, for a long moment. Hesitantly, he began to sift through the documents again.

"I'll let you think about it." Grogan got up to leave, then turned back. "Tuck, if you were listening to the radio to keep track of what was going on in Veil…what did you think when you heard about the recording?"

"What recording?"

Slowly, thoughtfully, she nodded. "Never mind."

* * *

Violet ducked. The knife whistled as it sliced the air overhead.

She dove toward the exit, wrenched the knob, and flung open the door. As she stepped on the threshold, she glanced down— and was glad she did. She turned her next step into a leap, knowing the killer was right behind her and hoping he wouldn't look toward his feet…

Violet sprawled on a dusty floor and flipped over onto her back. The killer loomed over her, raising the knife for a fatal stab—and dropped straight down through the hole in the floor.

Violet waited for a crash from below...but heard only silence.

Getting to her feet, she looked at where the door had existed a moment ago. It had swung closed after the killer came through, but now it was just a blank, crumbling wall. Violet recognized the inside of the abandoned building where Kurt Riner had held her hostage back in November. In a sense, it was the place where she had met—

"April!!" She turned on the spot and called again. Was April dead? Had an element of Violet's dream killed her? Could that actually happen to someone who wasn't even a real person? Violet found herself regretting the way she'd spoken to April in their final moments together. Secrets aside, all April had ever done was try to help Violet, and in return, she'd hurled mistrust and ire.

Why, before losing her memories, had Violet instructed April not to tell her her true identity? Had it been to protect herself? To protect someone else? Was it part of a plan? A necessary step to achieving a future goal? Perhaps Violet *was* meant to learn her identity, but only at a specific time in the future.

Or perhaps it was simply that Violet's past was too painful, and losing it was a blessing.

Violet turned and shuffled along the deteriorating hallway, wary of any other pitfalls. Even if she succeeded in finding out about her past, that knowledge would be lost to her the moment she woke up. That is, if she ever did wake up. The killer in this dream seemed determined to keep her from doing so. The quicker she got out of this building, the better.

Strangely, the building didn't seem as decrepit as the last time she was here. It was a wreck, but not as *much* of a wreck. Almost as if...

Violet stopped short. She heard movement up ahead. She

wished she had a flashlight. It was daytime, but the few windows that weren't obstructed by fallen debris were blackened with ash. She sidestepped over to a wall that seemed somewhat solid and put her back to it, listening hard. The last action proved unnecessary; whatever was making the noise wasn't adept at moving quietly. For a moment Violet thought it might be a frightened animal, its movements were so sporadic, its breathing treble, almost whimpering.

All at once it emerged into the hall, crawling through a small hole. But it wasn't an animal; it was a little girl, about eleven years old. She got to her feet unsteadily, looking up and down the hall, clearly lost and scared. She pawed long hair out of her face, which was smudged with dirt and tears.

Violet stared hard at the girl. She'd never seen her before, and yet... "Holy crap—Jen!!"

The girl shrieked and jumped so hard she stumbled and fell. *"Get away!"*

"No, no, no, no, it's okay! I'm a friend!" Violet put out her hands. "I'm not gonna hurt you! I promise! It's okay."

The girl's knees shook as she stood back up. She clung to a fallen I-beam for support.

"You're Jen, right? Jen Grogan?"

The girl gulped. "M-magenta."

"Right, of course." Violet's mind reeled. It was like being inside someone else's memory altogether. But when exactly was this? As a child, Jen had snuck into this building more than once.

"Who are you?" the girl squeaked.

"Well, um..."

"What are you doing here?"

Violet gave a half-shrug. "To be honest, I'm not sure. I don't even really know *how* I got here. I'm trying to get out, but I'm lost, like you. I, I don't know which way to go."

Magenta's legs had stopped shaking. She seemed less skittish but still wary.

"What about you?" asked Violet. "What brought you here?"

"I was trying to find my friend, V-violet."

This is the day Violet Hall was murdered. Which could only mean one thing.

A few weeks ago, Jen—adult Jen—had confessed to Violet a deep, underlying fear that not only was her childhood friend's killer still in Veil, but also, in fact, the serial killer. Violet had reassured her that with Kurt Riner behind bars, she could lay her fears to rest...but now it seemed Jen had been right after all. The serial killer had been active as long ago as Jen's tween years. Or had Riner been responsible for Violet Hall's death? Had he started the killing spree and then groomed someone to be his helper?

An ominous *creak* resounded from beyond the walls. Magenta gave a choked cry, scampered over to Violet, and clung to her arm.

No, Violet thought to herself with quiet certainty. *I'm here, seeing this Truth, because Violet Hall's killer...is* the *killer.*

"*She's dead!*" Magenta broke into sobs and wailed, "Violet's dead. He killed her."

Violet squatted and hugged the girl, felt her little body shaking. The Jen she knew from her present was such a bad-ass that, even having heard what had happened during her childhood, Violet had come to think of her as invulnerable, both physically and emotionally. Seeing her like this, she suddenly realized the little girl was still there, deep inside. "Oh, honey, I'm so sorry." She hugged her tighter.

Magenta buried her face in Violet's shoulder, so that when she spoke, her voice became muffled. "He's still here. He's still inside, with us."

"Yes, he is," Violet replied calmly.

"He's going to find us. He's going to kill us, too."

"No. He's not."

Magenta pulled back.

Resolution shone in Violet's amber eyes. "He's not going to kill you. Because I'm going to find out who he is. And I'm going to make sure he never hurts anyone, ever again."

They gazed at each other, and Magenta's sobs quieted. Then the girl's eyes looked over Violet's shoulder, and she went still as a statue.

Keeping her hand on Magenta's back, Violet got calmly to her feet and turned around. The killer stood at the far end of the hall, silhouetted against the opening to a stairwell where sunlight had broken through.

Without taking her eyes off the silhouette, Violet said to Magenta, "Go on." When the girl looked at her worriedly, she added, "It's okay. Go ahead." She flashed her a smile. "I got this."

The girl scrambled back into the hole in the wall through which she'd come.

Violet tilted her chin up. "So! Who are you, then?"

VIII

The hospital was quiet. Some of the staff were still on duty, but the hallway outside Violet's room was empty. No one had traversed from either end for several minutes.

Deputy Derrick's feet were sore, yet he continued to remain standing by the door. The truth was, he was too stunned to notice the pain. Sheriff Dubowski was gone, killed, and not in the line of duty, but because he'd been trying to commit a double murder—to cover up yet another crime. The other deputies—apart from Hayden, who'd been sent home—were all neck-deep in busywork, processing their feelings through activity. But Derrick didn't want to process anything. He wanted to...

Derrick turned his head and peered through the small window in the door. From this angle, he could see Violet sleeping soundly. If Grogan was right, then the only reason things were different now, the reason Dubowski was dead and disgraced, was that Violet had gone into that little store at the same time he did. If she hadn't been there...

If she had never come to Veil in the first place...

Violet stirred. Was she waking up?

Derrick's mind went back to an earlier conversation: *"I can't tell them anything until Violet wakes up and confirms what the evidence is saying."*

Violet's head gave a little twitch.

Derrick looked up and down the hall. Still quiet, still empty. He turned the handle of the door and went inside.

* * *

Violet's fist pounded against the door. She glanced behind herself again and again to make sure she didn't get ambushed. Finally, the front door of the house was answered by an elderly lady. "Hi," Violet said breathlessly. "Sharon Brisbon? My name's Violet. I'm guessing this is the night you die, and I'm also guessing it wasn't an accident, you were murdered by the serial killer. He's after me now, but that's okay because I'm after him, too. Although even if I find out who he is, I'll still forget as soon as I wake up from this dream, but I guess, one problem at a time."

Sharon stood there, flummoxed and gawking, until a sharp *tap-tap-tap* sounded behind her.

"That'll be him." Violet pushed past her.

Sharon's living room had a large glass sliding door overlooking her back deck and yard. When Violet drew aside the blinds, Sharon yelped at the sight of the masked phantom beyond the glass.

"Oh, come on!" Violet chided him. "Again with the stupid mask! I know you weren't wearing one that night—why would you? So that's cheating!"

"Y-you!" White as a sheet, Sharon backed against a table and pointed a shaking finger. "It's you!!"

Violet looked from Sharon to the killer. "Are you kidding me? *She* can see who you are but I can't? That's just unfair."

"How can it be you?!" Sharon wailed. "You're *dead!!"*

Violet blinked. "Wait—what?"

The killer's fist smashed through the glass. Violet shielded her face from the exploding shards, then dodged as the killer slashed at her with the knife. How was she supposed to pull his mask off when she couldn't get close to him?

The killer made another swipe. Violet darted across the room—and tripped over Sharon, who had fainted dead away. She felt his footsteps pounding toward her...

At the last moment, she rolled onto her back and struck with the shard of glass clutched in her fingers. The shard sliced the killer's hand and the knife flew across the room.

Violet rose off the floor and launched herself at the killer. The force of her tackle knocked them both through the shattered doorway and into the darkness.

* * *

Cy and her mother watched from the waiting area in the hospital lobby as Deputy Benno escorted Tuck Fleagle away. "So," said the girl, "he never actually knew who Violet is. He just thought he did."

Jen nodded with a wry smile. "Just a coincidence. Violet happened to fit a character in his...in the story he'd invented."

Cy wrinkled her nose. "That's kind of a letdown. After all these months of trying to find him."

"Agreed."

"But then who was trying to get into Violet's hospital room?"

Jen sighed. "We've swept the hospital twice. Tuck was the only unauthorized person here. Visiting hours are well over, and the hospital staff are on the lookout for anyone who isn't a patient, a deputy, or one of their own."

"Or me," Cy added, knowing her mother had made a special request that she be allowed to stay.

"And even if someone did manage to sneak in and evade the searches, they couldn't have known where Violet was sleeping without—" She broke off.

Cy frowned. "Mom?"

Jen's brow was creased, a sign that the wheels in her head were spinning. "Violet was put in that room second," she murmured. "We assumed Violet was the target because she was alone when someone tried to…" She grabbed her radio. "Grogan to Derrick." Silence. "Grogan to Derrick, come in!"

Growing frightened, Cy said, "Mom—"

But Sheriff Grogan had already taken off down the hall.

* * *

Moonlight shone down on the village square in the center of Veil. Violet and the killer tumbled over and over in the snow, locked in a tangle of jabs and strangleholds. Of all the theories Violet had come up with as to her identity, "secret agent" was one of the first she'd discarded. She was no fighter. But she didn't let that dampen her ferocity.

"Who are you?!" she screamed, clawing at his mask and digging her knee into his midsection. With a snarl, the killer rolled her onto her back, pinning her arms to the ground. For an instant he held her there, staring down at her, snorting bestially. Violet's head shot upward—and the killer hollered in agony. Violet had meant to snag the mask with her teeth, but she'd ended up biting his chin. Violet tried to focus on the screams: was that really a man's voice or—

The killer slammed his head into hers, then he sprang off of her. Violet opened her smarting eyes and found it was daytime. They were in Riverbend Park.

"No!!!" Violet shot to her feet and sprinted after him. "I am not letting you go!"

The killer was too fast. He was outdistancing her—but then suddenly he halted.

Violet sped up, and with a leap she clobbered him—and she realized why he'd stopped. Together they toppled headfirst into the river.

* * *

"Grogan to all deputies!" The sheriff swung around a corner and barely avoided tripping over a water cooler. "I need immediate backup at the hospital, room two-twenty!" She skidded to a halt and vaulted up the stairs.

* * *

Violet and the killer crashed onto a polished floor beneath flashing lights of different colors. Loud, upbeat music boomed from several speakers. This was the dance club Violet had visited last November.

Violet made a swipe at the killer, but her aim was off from her disorientation. The killer didn't seem to suffer so: his punch landed right on the side of her head. She wobbled but didn't fall. The killer turned, and Violet thought he was going to run again—till he swung the other way and backhanded her. A third blow knocked her off her feet, and before she could get back up, his foot thudded down onto her neck. She grabbed his ankle and twisted it, pummeled at his shin, but his leg wouldn't budge. She could feel him crushing her windpipe, just as Dubowski had, and knowing this was a dream didn't help her. It felt real enough.

Mouth wide open as she tried to suck in air, she looked up and saw him staring down at her, as he had before. She understood: he wanted the last thing she saw to be his covered face, so that her last thought would be—*I failed.*

Then something charged into the light and caught the killer

by surprise. As Violet gasped for breath, the killer pivoted to face his new opponent—and something clipped him in the back of the head.

Wheezing, Violet got to her feet. She stared in wonder at her two rescuers...

They were Marcy Temple and Rob Mulroy. Both regarded the killer, wearing smoldering expressions.

The killer seemed to hear something and pivoted again. Only the center of the large room was illuminated; the outer edges were in shadow. Into the light, from different directions, stepped three more people: Matt Foley, Amy Chester, and Byron Temple. All his other Veil victims apart from Sharon Brisbon.

Mutely they formed a circle around the killer. There was no need for them to speak; their eyes said it all.

The killer spun this way and that, seeking an escape that wasn't there.

Violet found her voice and barked, "Do it!!"

The dead fell upon their murderer savagely, brutally. Violet thought perhaps she should turn away, but she didn't.

When the killer's legs gave way, the five victims took hold of him, securing his arms. Then, creepily, as one, they all looked up at Violet.

Unsteadily she walked toward her nemesis, who raised his head.

Violet reached out.

Slowly he shook his head from side to side, as if in warning. As if to say, *You really don't want to know.*

Violet lowered her hand. "I might never know my name," she said mildly. "But at least now...*I'll know yours!*"

She seized the mask and ripped it off.

A startled cry escaped her lips.

The killer's face broke into a grin.

Violet shook her head, trembling all over. "What...no..."

The killer began to laugh.

"You... *How can it be you??!*"

The laugh became a cackle. The same cackle Violet had heard after Rob was shot.

"HOW CAN IT BE YOU?!!!"

The cackle died down. "Oh, Violet. I *told* you there was a connection between us."

"But—why???"

"I...made...a *PROMISE!!!!*"

* * *

The door of the recovery room was unguarded. Sheriff Grogan peeked through the small window, saw what she expected to see, and opened the door, her hand on her sidearm.

As calmly as she could, she said, "Deputy..."

Violet was still asleep. But Deputy Derrick wasn't standing by Violet's bed. He was standing at the foot of Joy's, with his back to the door. Joy was sitting ramrod straight, with a terrified look on her face.

"Deputy Derrick, I need you to turn around and face me." His hand, she could see, also hovered by his sidearm.

But he didn't turn around. "I'm kind of in the middle of something, Grogan," he said in a low voice.

"James, we can talk about this. I know you're in shock over Dubowski's death. All of us are. We can talk about it. But first I need you to—"

"Sheriff, I'm gonna need *you* to take another step."

"What?"

"Take another step into the room."

"Why?"

"Because I don't think you can see what's really going on."

That was when Grogan noticed Joy wasn't looking at Derrick. Her eyes were fixed on something much closer to her.

Grogan took another step...

And the person Derrick's tall figure had been blocking from view became visible. It was a woman in a hoodie, holding a hypodermic syringe.

"Hayden?! What are you doing?"

"Apparently, what you thought *I* was doing," Derrick said dryly.

* * *

Violet was still shaking her head. "This doesn't make sense!"

"Makes no difference," the killer said smugly. "You're just going to forget about it once you wake up."

Violet peered into the killer's eyes. "Then why are you after me?" She pointed in realization. "It's because I'm close, isn't it! Out there, in the real world, I've found all the clues I need in order to figure out who you are."

The killer had stopped smiling.

"You were never afraid of me finding you out in here. You're afraid of me *out there,* aren't you."

The killer began moving jerkily, trying to break free.

Violet blew out a deep breath of contentment. "I'm going to wake up," she said. "I'm going to find out who you really are. I'm going to stop you." And then, because she couldn't help it: "I'm going to make sure *you don't keep your promise.*"

With that she turned and marched away.

She had only made it a few steps before she heard a deep, guttural roar, building in pitch and volume. She turned back to see the killer uttering the cry, getting louder by the moment.

Suddenly the ground began shaking, quaking. The five people restraining the killer lost their grip as they struggled to keep their balance.

With a mighty jolt, the killer broke free.

Violet dashed toward the door by a glowing EXIT sign. Acting on impulse, she went through and immediately locked the door behind her.

Only then did she notice she was still in the building. In a restroom, to be specific.

"Oh, come on!!"

She jumped as something crashed against the door from the other side. Then again, and again. The killer was battering it down, one impact at a time. It shook the whole room.

But there was another sound. A low, desperate moan. "V-violet…"

Violet turned to see someone lying in the corner. "Oh my god—April!!"

IX

"Hayden… Jessica, drop the needle and move away from the bed."

"I'm not listening to anything you say, *Deputy* Grogan!" Hayden's eyes were fixed on Joy, who shrank as far away from her as she could.

"You do not want to do this," said Grogan, a biting edge to her voice.

"Someone has to get justice for the sheriff! If you won't—"

"This isn't justice, this is murder!"

"She killed him!!" Hayden trembled with rage.

"He…" Joy's voice shook. She didn't see Grogan frantically shaking her head. "He was a rapist. He tried to kill me—"

"Then he *should* have!" shrieked Hayden. "Your whole family is a sick, twisted embarrassment to this town! We did you all a favor by letting you stay, and you took away our best man. You little…diseased…"

"Hayden." Deputy Derrick chanced a step forward. "I was trying to tell you—I'm angry, too. I'm furious at this woman. But killing her is wrong. That's not the way to show your loyalty."

Hayden let out a disturbed chuckle. "Loyalty? You think *your* loyalty means anything? Your idiocy has been shaming us—

shaming *him*—ever since you joined us. You think Grogan's the reason you got passed over for senior deputy? The sheriff was so embarrassed by you, you were never even in the running."

A vein pulsed in Derrick's forehead. "He...he wouldn't have wanted you to do this."

Hayden's eyes glistened. "I know," she sobbed. "He was a good man." Her head swiveled and as she looked again at Joy, her voice hardened. "And good men have to be avenged."

* * *

"April!" Violet cupped the beautiful woman's face in her hands. April's eyelids fluttered droopily. "April, I'm sorry I yelled at you, I'm sorry for everything, but you have to tell me—how do I remember???"

The pounding on the door began to intensify. Wood began to splinter.

"After I wake up, how do I remember what I've seen?!"

April opened her mouth. "M...mi..."

"What?"

"M-mirror..."

"Mirror??"

"Mir..." April's head lolled.

BAM! BAM!

Violet looked around frantically—and zeroed in on the mirror above the sink.

BAM! BAM! BAM!

She darted over to it and nearly touched noses with her reflection. "Mirror...mirror... What am I supposed to—"

She shrieked as the next blow popped one of the hinges off the door. It flew across the room; she ducked, and it cracked the mirror across the middle.

She looked in the mirror again—and recoiled with a yelp.

Gone was her reflection! In its place she saw an image of herself, but she was lying in a hospital bed, asleep.

CRACK!

"Wake up!" Violet shouted. "You have to wake up! You have to remember!"

CRACK! The door began to separate from the wall.

"Please! Remember!!"

CRACK!

"Remember!!!"

CRACK—the door came down—

"Remem—"

* * *

Grogan drew her sidearm. "This is your last warning, Hayden. I won't let you do this."

Indecision peeked out from Hayden's streaming eyes. "I *have* to!"

Grogan clicked off the safety. "Put—it—down."

A trembling Joy shut her eyes.

Derrick shook his head at Hayden pleadingly.

Hayden gulped…and drew a quick breath—

Violet shot up in her bed across the room and screeched, *"REMEMBER!!!!!"*

Everyone jumped. The needle flew from Hayden's hand. In an instant, Grogan was on her, Derrick assisting a moment later.

Violet's head fell back onto the pillow. She tried to say, "What happened?" but her throat was too sore.

* * *

"I remembered what Bethany said about her kidnapper, and I realized it was him." Violet's voice was hoarse and scratchy. She grimaced as she spoke. "Then he started talking about Kristy.

The things he said... I think he was gonna go after her next. It was horrible."

Joy had been released from the hospital. Violet had confirmed her story. Sheriff Grogan, Deputy Derrick, and Cy were by Violet's hospital bed. Cy was holding her hand.

"When he turned around and saw me, I didn't say anything, but my face must have given me away." She hesitated.

"You don't have to go over what happened after that," said Grogan. Violet sank back, relieved.

"Do you want some water?" asked Cy.

Violet shook her head. "When can I go home?"

"I have some things I have to take care of right away," the sheriff said heavily, "so why don't you get some rest and I'll see if I can get you released this afternoon."

"I can't believe it's morning," said Cy. Then she yawned an immense yawn and amended, "Maybe I can."

Derrick followed Grogan into the hall. "You're gonna tell the public now?"

"The first thing I have to do is tell Bethany Williams her abductor won't be bothering her again. *Then* I'll tell the public about Dubowski...and Hayden." She paused and shut her eyes. "This is going to be rough."

Derrick cleared his throat. "You can count on my support, for what it's worth."

Grogan looked at him and raised an eyebrow.

"The man I was loyal to—I mean, the man I thought he was— might not have ever existed, but I can still honor that man by doing my duty. And I'll try not to embarrass anyone."

"Thanks," Grogan said wryly. She started down the hall, then paused again. "Just one thing: how did Hayden get into the recovery room?"

"Well, the hospital staff didn't know you'd taken Hayden off duty, so they didn't report her as an unauthorized person."

"Yes, I know," Grogan said patiently, "but you were still stationed outside the room."

A blank look appeared in Derrick's eyes. "Oh," he said. A few seconds passed, then he went on, "Oh, yeah, I saw Violet moving around and I thought she was waking up, so I went into the room to check on her. Hayden must have thought the coast was clear. She was halfway across the room before she noticed me."

Grogan nodded slowly. "Well, next time, just call a nurse."

"Will do."

* * *

"Are you hungry for anything?" asked Cy.

Violet gestured feebly to her throat and rasped, "Maybe something with honey."

"Sure." Cy gave her a quick hug, then she went to the door. Stepping into the hall, she said, "Oh!" and smiled. She held the door open for Candy, who looked as if she'd barely slept.

Violet sat up and tried to say, "Hi!" It came out sounding like a hairball.

"Hey," said Candy timidly. "Are you…"

"I'm fine!" Violet rasped.

"Good." Candy glanced back.

"Oh, sorry." Cy left the doorway.

Candy stood awkwardly beside Violet's bed. Before Violet could attempt another sentence, Candy said, "I owe you an apology."

"What? No, I—" She coughed. "I messed up."

Candy gave her a pained look. "Maybe, but I had no right to shout at you like that, and definitely not to compare you to my mother." She put a hand over her eyes. "I accused you of not being there for me, but I never even thought to ask you if you were on board with helping Bethany, and you stuck with me through everything!"

"It's okay!" Violet caught Candy's hand and squeezed it. "It's okay. You were in pain. I get it."

Candy sat and looked at Violet with watery eyes. "Even when I'm hurting, you can tell me when I'm out of line. And I promise I'll try not to get like that again. Will you forgive me?"

Violet's own eyes watered with joy as she nodded. "You—forgive me?"

Candy rolled her eyes impishly and grinned. "I forgave you, like, fifty times, sitting here, you just weren't listening."

Violet lay back with a raspy chuckle and gazed blissfully.

Candy glanced down. "Um…how badly does your face hurt?"

Violet reached over and kissed her.

Eavesdropping from just outside the door, Cy pumped her fist and went off to procure some breakfast.

She was crossing the lobby when someone called her name. She turned and went stock-still.

Her friends, Em and Neesha, had just passed through the entrance.

Neesha approached first. "Hey," she said tentatively. "Is Violet okay?"

Cy stared at her and said nothing.

"Look, I just wanted to say I'm sorry. I shouldn't have iced you out. And I wasn't totally honest with you about why I was angry. It took me a while to admit—it wasn't your fault. I would've talked to you sooner, I just didn't know what to say. When I got the invite to your sleepover, I just sort of froze up. And Em only put off talking to you because I hadn't yet."

Cy still said nothing.

"Anyway, I got a phone call last night from that weird lady, Myrna Redpath. She said you were dealing with some heavy stuff and needed your friends, so…" She gestured helplessly. "We're—here, for what it's worth."

Em, who had been hovering a few feet behind, finally stepped up. "We miss you."

"Yeah. And we wanna work things out, if that's cool with you."

Cy swallowed, starting to fume.

Neesha glanced at Em. "It doesn't have to be right now," she said. "Just wanted to open the door." She started to turn away.

"Why did you do it?!"

Neesha turned back and frowned. "Excuse me?"

"Why did you send me that email?"

Em and Neesha exchanged confused glances. "What email?"

Cy was quickly dissolving into angry tears. "You said… You sent me an email saying my mom… You said my mom…"

"Hey, whoa, Cy…" Neesha gently took her by the shoulders. "I don't know what you're talking about. I didn't send you an email."

Cy broke down completely. Neesha hugged her and soothed her.

Epilogue

"Mayor Pressler speaking."

"Good afternoon, Mr. Mayor."

"Sheriff Grogan. I figured you must have your hands full, so I didn't want to bother you, but I'm truly sorry for your department's loss. It's a tragic loss to the town as well. If there's anything my office can do for you—"

"Not to be rude, Mr. Mayor, but you're right, I am busy, and I don't have time for sentimentality or platitudes. I need to ask you two things."

"Of course."

"As you probably know, we found Tuck Fleagle."

"I did hear a rumor. Has he been able to help you? Did he tell you anything useful?"

"Nothing we were hoping for."

"That's unfortunate."

"But he did mention one thing I found surprising. It turns out, this whole time, he's been living in a cabin just a few miles from Veil."

"Living off the grid, eh?"

"Not completely. He had a radio. He listened to our public station. Except that his radio cut out once—exactly once—and he missed the broadcast about the recording of him and Rob Mulroy, made just before Rob's murder. Now, if he'd heard that broadcast, he might've come forward a long time ago, but because his radio cut out that one time, he didn't."

"Well—"

And it occurred to me, there have been other times certain radios have inexplicably gone dead at conspicuous moments. Like the night my house was broken into, during the curfew. Or when my family and I were lost in the woods, trying to get little Megan Toombs back to safety. It's almost as if someone has been deliberately jamming radio signals, but I don't know anyone who has the equipment to do that. Do you?

"No, I'm afraid I don't."

"Hm. Oh well."

"What was the second thing you wanted to ask me?"

"Oh, yes. Did you send my daughter an email purporting to be one of her high school friends?"

"I beg your pardon?"

"My daughter received an email that made her quite upset. It was faked to look like it came from one of her classmates."

"This is completely inapprop—"

"And Violet, now that she's awake, tells me you threatened her yesterday morning. Something to the effect of: 'What's about to happen is your fault.' Did you attempt to hurt her by driving a rift between me and my daughter, thereby breaking apart Violet's family?"

"That is slander! You can't prove—"

"My daughter's right here, if you'd like to explain it to her."

"Hello, Mr. Pressler."

For five seconds, Pressler stayed on the line, jaw twitching, before he slammed down the receiver. Then he grabbed the whole phone and threw it across the room for good measure.

* * *

"I've got this bad feeling."

"About what?" asked Candy. She was snuggling Violet in her hospital bed, their faces inches apart.

"It feels like I've forgotten something. Something important."

"Doesn't sound like you."

Frowning to herself, Violet asked, "Did I—talk at all while I was asleep?"

"Yeah, you did, actually."

Violet lifted her head a little. "What did I say?"

Candy winced. "I couldn't understand most of it."

Violet dropped her head back down in disappointment.

Candy, still thinking, amended, "Actually there was one word I understood. I remember because you said it a few times."

"What word?"

"'Mirror.'"

Violet blinked. "Mirror?" She turned her head and stared up at the ceiling in puzzlement. "Mirror…"

WINTER IN VEIL

A Mystery Novella Series
by Miles Ledoux

Next time in Veil...

"Sit down, Mr. Browning," the sheriff ordered, unruffled by his outburst. When he obeyed, she went back to her chair and sat opposite him. "I apologize for the rigorous questioning. Since Violet came to Veil, I've assumed responsibility for her wellbeing. I...I've grown to care for her. I'm sure you can understand that."

Browning gave a nod, looking slightly mollified.

"So you can also understand that when a stranger appears out of the blue, claiming to be her family, I feel obligated to ask for proof before—"

"Proof? You want proof?" Browning pulled a manila envelope from his jacket pocket. With trembling hands, he handed it to Grogan.

Benno sidled over as Grogan opened the envelope and drew out a wad of photographs. The first was of two people standing beside a wooden sign that read, *Summit: 2,454 feet*. Beyond them was a beautiful, lush mountain vista.

The two people were Wade Browning...and Violet, with his arm around her shoulders.

About the Author

Miles Ledoux was born in upstate New York and started writing murder mysteries at the age of nine. His first paid writing gig was in 2007, when a local theatre chose one of his plays for their summer melodrama. He received other royalties after moving to Los Angeles for graduate school, where he wrote, directed, and produced several mystery dessert theatre plays. He also started a side business designing and running mystery party games while working as a martial arts instructor.

Currently the author resides in Springfield, Vermont. Despite having lived in five different states, he has remained active in community theatre as a playwright, director, and actor. He also has a YouTube channel where he compares Agatha Christie adaptations to the books they were based on. His handle is @MysteryMiles.

Miles loves books, cats, music, Star Trek, Peanuts, and owns an ever-growing number of variations of the board game Clue. His favorite author is Lloyd Alexander.

You can connect with me on:

🌐 https://www.ledouxmysteries.com